GET THESE MEN OUT OF THE HOT SUN

Also by Herbert Mitgang

FICTION

THE RETURN

BIOGRAPHY

ABRAHAM LINCOLN: A PRESS PORTRAIT
(Lincoln as They Saw Him)
THE MAN WHO RODE THE TIGER:
The Life and Times of Judge Samuel Seabury

CRITICISM

WORKING FOR THE READER: A Chronicle of Culture,
Literature, War and Politics in Books
from the 1950's to the Present

REPORTAGE

FREEDOM TO SELL:
Television and the First Amendment

EDITED BY HERBERT MITGANG

THE LETTERS OF CARL SANDBURG
AMERICA AT RANDOM: Topics of *The Times*
WASHINGTON, D. C., IN LINCOLN'S TIME (by Noah Brooks)
CIVILIANS UNDER ARMS: Stars and Stripes, Civil War to Korea
SPECTATOR OF AMERICA (by Edward Dicey)

GET THESE MEN
OUT OF
THE HOT SUN

by Herbert Mitgang

ARBOR HOUSE

NEW YORK

Library of Congress Catalog Card Number: 71–188941
ISBN: 0–87795–035–0

Manufactured in the United States of America

Acknowledgment is gratefully made to Donald I. Fine, president and publisher of Arbor House, for astute editorial guidance.

The events in this story all take place several years in the future. Obviously, then, the characters and their ex cathedra remarks are invented and bear no relationship to alleged living persons, though some actual public names and countries and wars are used for historical reference. The President and Vice President in particular have no basis in reality; nor is their *country to be confused with the United States.*

Contents

PART I   THE WOUNDED COUNTRY

    1. The State of the Union, 1976   11
    2. The Shrinking of Richie Nixon   35
    3. The State of Spiro Agnewism   53

PART II   THE K. PLAN

    4. Box 1944   91
    5. The Trojan Horse   109
    6. On the White House Team   131

PART III   THE BODY COUNT

    7. Conventions and Election   159
    8. President-elect Agnew   177
    9. January 20, 1977   195
    10. An Old Republic   203

PART I

THE WOUNDED COUNTRY

CHAPTER 1

The State of the Union, 1976

As WARS go, the war in Burma wasn't much but it was
cherished by the President and the Pentagon because it
was the only war they had at the moment that they could
call their very own. On Christmas Eve, 1975, the White
House telecommunications *apparat* mounted a pictur-
esque three-hour spectacular on its Good News Hour
entitled "Over There—The New Spirit of '76." It was a
tribute by President Nixon and Vice President Agnew to
the grunts dug in along the banks of the Irrawaddy.

"Tonight our boys are getting turkey and all the
fixin's," the unseen President's voice narrated while color
cameras closed in on sampans carrying dressed birds up-
river. "Let me conclude, my fellow Americans, by offering our solemn prayers in the name of the Prince of
Peace and of the United States for the freedom we both
symbolize. From the rude bridge at Lexington to the
rice fields of Rangoon, our Minutemen have been there.
Now I pledge that your menfolk will be eating turkey at

home by next Christmas, under my new program of phased withdrawals from Asia."

But it took awhile for the American press, including something silly called broadcast journalism, to notice that the voiceover was headless; that strange things were happening inside the White House unparalleled since the declining days of Woodrow Wilson's Presidency.

The first hint came on New Year's Day, 1976, in a column by I. F. Stone titled "The Evil of Banality." After the 1973 inauguration, he had decided to revive his newsletter in Toronto. *I. F. Stone's Weekly-in-Exile* read:

"The trial of Adolf Eichmann for making the concentration camp trains run on time and filling the death quotas proved—in Hannah Arendt's phrase—the banality of evil. As the seventh year of the Nixon-Agnew Administration draws to another sorry end, and all efforts are pointed toward their perpetuation in next November's presidential election, Americans below this border face the strongest possibility—now that the Constitutional limitation on the Presidency has been revised—that their lives will be controlled for another four years beyond January 20, 1977, by these two shallow individuals who personify what is disastrous for republican government and the United States itself—the evil of banality."

But of much greater meaning was the observation he threw out almost casually at the end of his article:

"PS: I wonder if my former colleagues in the Washington press corps have noticed that Nixon has not had any real contact with the public in the last half-year or so? No live press conferences, no live speeches before Republican gatherings, no live visits to any major American city? It's never happened up to now—can it mean something more than the usual manipulation of the media that is the hallmark of the Nixon-Agnew regime?"

Stone's hint was first picked up and illustrated by Bill Mauldin in the *Chicago Sun-Times* and later reprinted in the *New Republic* and the *Progressive.* His drawing showed the White House as an airplane soaring over the Washington Monument, its four whirling propellors all wearing the grinning likeness of Spiro T. Agnew. On the ground, two Air Force colonels look up at the mission overhead and remark in Mauldin's caption line: "One of our Presidents is missing."

He was, and he wasn't.

Richard Milhous Nixon was indeed in the White House but he had stopped functioning as President of the United States except ceremonially.

The American public still received the impression that he was actively holding the reins of government. Presidential messages were delivered regularly to Congress,

13

at even greater length than in the first term of his Administration. Appointments were made in his name as disgruntled members of the Cabinet resigned because their authority was usurped by opposite numbers in the White House inner circle of counselors. The letters of acceptance were gracefully written and signed—some students of the Presidency felt almost too casually for the dignity of the Office of Chief Executive—with an ingratiating "Dick." Foreign dignitaries were received in the Rose Garden, ambassadors coming and going had their hands shaken under the portico, Cotton Bowl queens and prize-winning women golfers were dutifully kissed, and, while David Eisenhower and his former college chums tossed a football on the White House lawn, official pictures were released showing his father-in-law waving in the background.

All this noble silence and lack of bellicosity was greeted by commentators as a sign of the President's deepening sense of his role. Several times every week TV analysts on all three network news shows described the new Nixon stance as "statesmanlike." In *Newsweek*, Stewart Alsop wrote approvingly, "Low Profile at the White House." Over Hugh Sidey's Presidency column in *Life*, the headline declared: "A Time of Moderation, a Time of Deliberation."

Actually, it was a time of turmoil but it was almost totally invisible. Much of the credit for the concealment

14

could be given to a handful of communications special-
ists around Nixon, including the professionals who had
helped to recast his image from bearded sorehead to
political statesman during his second term. These condottieri behaved like loyal mercenaries serving an ambitious
prince in fourteenth-century Italy: given the ducats of
the realm and wearing the prestigious doublets of White
House favor, they were surprisingly faithful to their
liege even when it became apparent that he had turned
into a windup doll.

But he was *their* windup doll, and that made all the
difference. At least temporarily Nixon's mechanical responses were programmed to indicate greater activity
on the administrative level—visits to the Bureau of
Printing and Engraving to double check on the proper
size of the people's money ("We in this Administration
will not shortchange the public through smaller dollars," the press release said afterward) and to make sure
that no radical elements had changed the traditional
language on Federal Reserve notes ("So long as I am
President," he was said to have said, after a Sunday
morning service led by the Reverend Dr. Billy Graham
live and in person, "the imperishable phrase *In God We
Trust* will not be erased from the escutcheon of your
currency"); visits to the Smithsonian Institution ("This
great little monoplane flown by Lucky Lindy across the
Atlantic stands for more than the *Spirit of St. Louis*—it

15

symbolizes the spirit of individual progress permitted in the Age of Coolidge and," he told two surprised guards and several tourists, "that selfsame attitude toward the inherent right of private achievement can make your sons astronauts in what some historians are already calling the Age of Nixon"); visits to the $150 million structure on Pennsylvania Avenue—which Murray Kempton in the *New York Review of Books* nicknamed "The Cops' Pentagon"—serving as headquarters for the Federal Bureau of Investigation ("The banks of computers here are able to punch up the names and records of anyone who has ever received a ticket for making a U-turn on his respective Main Street, a tribute to scientific police progress and," Mr. Nixon declared in unprepared remarks, "a personal tribute to my old friend and colleague, J. Edgar Hoover, a fine Director, a generous human being and, last but never least, a loyal sports fan").

It took some doing to keep up appearances but the media group around the President confidently managed to keep him under wraps. They spoke each other's language. All had originally worked in advertising or television, all were true believers in their ability to persuade large numbers of people through the controlled small screen, and all had first call upon the powers in broadcasting whose licenses were subject to approval by the all-seeing Counselor of Telecommunications at the

White House. Ronald Ziegler, former press secretary, had been offered the powerful spot but had opted to return to his old employer, Disneyland. The Telecommunications Office remained without a formal chief, enabling all the others in the *apparat* to put the heat on through it. Frank Shakespeare, whose former career as a network time salesman and station manager had led to his appointment as Republican party telepolitical consultant, head of the United States Information Agency and the Voice of America, actually spent most of his days and night monitoring alleged wisecracks against the Nixnew Administration. Richard Kleindienst, nicknamed "Genghis Khan" because of his ability to control troops of delegates in political as well as veterans' conventions, devoted his energies to keeping the ambitious jackals led by Governor Ronald Reagan and his well-oiled Southwestern friends from closing in on the President. Herman Heinz, a token good guy, acted as emissary to the entertainment and dwindling cultural industries, arranging for grants, lecture tours, and artistic ventures for creative people and troupes who behaved themselves. Herbert Klein served as *Capo* of all Cabinet and federal agency press officers, most of whom were known in Washington's own Mafia slang as his "button" men, keeping an eye on underlings whose loyalties to Nixon wavered. But the most overbearing of these Rhine handmaidens with Teutonic manners was H. R. Haldeman, formerly of the J. Walter Thompson advertising agency, who proudly liked to describe himself as "Dick's S.O.B."

Haldeman controlled the gate to the White House and the presidential nonpresence. In this capacity he screened the press and used its executives to suppress their own too-inquiring reporters. He had two simple card files on most of the writers and editors and commentators in journalism and broadcasting: the first was called "With Us," the second "Against Us." Rarely could someone on his wrong list be reinstated to good graces; stories considered unfavorable years ago—going back to Nixon's days as a congressional Red-hunter—could be summoned quickly on his hot line to the FBI. In this respect, the President's own memory of real and imagined slights was reliable in the extreme.

Only two publications could be trusted at all times and serve as semiofficial conduits for presidential handouts—*TV Guide* and *CATV Digest,* the new magazine for community antenna shows. Walter Annenberg, the horse racing and television publisher, had been able to hold onto his ambassadorship to the Court of St. James by making further contributions to the victorious Nixon-Agnew campaign in '72. Rolf Minton, the publisher and top editorial policy maker at *CATV Digest,* had reprinted the speeches of Nixon and Agnew and paid them handsomely as honorary contributing editors. Both mass-circulation telemagazines had begun to print articles about personal uplift and political affairs; both praised the client-states that formed the nucleus of the Nixon Doctrine.

Unfortunately, that doctrine had failed to extricate all the American troops from Southeast Asia before the promised deadlines that were always being revised. New sanctuaries had to be destroyed somewhere before the monsoon season started. Indeed, the monsoon desk in the Pentagon played the rainy weather two ways in drawing up its Asian calculations: if a new attack was planned as part of any withdrawal scheme, it was mounted just in time to close in before the jungles became impassable; if any revolutionaries launched a counterattack during the monsoon season when presumably they had been stymied, it was attributed to their inability to come out in the open high ground and fight any longer. The supplemental authority quoted at the National War College was not Clausewitz but *Alice in Wonderland,* with the Command and General Staff College providing graduate reading in *Through the Looking-Glass.* At the same time that men were withdrawn with great fanfare, replacements were delivered to several shaky contiguous countries.

When correspondents reported increases in the number of holes in the ground caused by B-52 bombers and more areas liberated by chemical herbicides made in U.S.A., Haldeman, Kleindienst, Shakespeare, and company mounted communications counterattacks. Instead of trying to discredit the reporters, they mousetrapped their publishers and network executives and affiliates. It was done by carefully timed invitations to the White House off-the-record dinners with the President. The executives would often find themselves sitting next to the biggest space and time buyers—automobile manufacturers, drug and soap moguls, insurance company directors—for the lecture delivered by Mr. Agnew on the need for "objectivity." The Vice President—who by now was Acting President in all but name—had memorized a handful of quotations about the First Amendment which impressed the executives mightily. His favorite was half compliment, half warning. "As Napoleon Bonaparte once said," grinned Spiro Agnew, "a journalist is a grumbler, a censurer, a giver of advice, a regent of sovereigns, a tutor of nations." He always ended with his clincher: "As long as I am here *your* First Amendment freedoms will be guarded—and I hope you will respect *mine,* too."

Anybody who could quote Napoleon couldn't be all bad, and most of the executives left the White House stag dinners resolved to tell their broadcast managers and editors that, in person and once you got to know him, Agnew was really something of an intellectual but had to talk the way he did for political expediency. The favorite word brought back to New York, Chicago, and

Los Angeles was *shrill:* "From here on out let's play him straight," said the president of NBC News to his correspondents, "and call the shots without being *shrill.*" Meaning, said David Brinkley under his breath to a colleague, "When Agnew opens his mouth, you close yours."

There was only one slight hitch at these presidential stag dinners: the President was seldom there. The usual procedure was for him to show up at the beginning for a quick, surrounded handshake (photographed and later proudly hung in the media executive's office), smile much and say as little as possible, and then be whisked away for an unexpected crisis of state. The Vice President, waiting in the wings, would then make his appearance. Before the guests knew what really was happening, Agnew would be off and running on his favorite epigram of the week. And as they milled around for his Mencken *manqué* gems to take back to the office, he always gave *his booboisie* a good show by complaining about the senators who belonged to the "Radic-Lib Eastern Establishment."

Now I. F. Stone began hitting his suspected theme of the missing President almost every issue. In spite of the restraints placed upon them by their publishers—who liked to stress that their newspapers had an obligation to be not merely free but, more important, something known as "responsible"—other columnists began to call

21

for visible press conferences. An editorial in the *St. Louis Post-Dispatch*, one of the few remaining papers openly using the weapons of sarcasm and wit against the Nixnew Government, demanded monthly accountings by the Chief Executive while Americans continued to die in Southeast Asia. To no avail.

Early in 1976, Messrs. Haldeman, Kleindienst, and Klein of the President's communications *apparat* began to panic. The President was in no condition to face the leaders of his own political party, let alone the press. They had stalled Senator Strom Thurmond of South Carolina repeatedly when he insisted on seeing Nixon in person, alone. For the hundreth time, Thurmond had told them, "You boys know that I delivered the Deep South in '68 and '72 and I'm the only one can do it again in '76. Ol' Strom is the man stands between political disaster and Georgie Wallace. I want to see Dick and talk about what some of your civil rights lawyers are doing to our schools. I have Mitchell's word that things are going to slow down—and I want it from the Man hisself. Otherwise—"

They reassured Thurmond that the Man was totally committed to his way of thinking, and that the school thing was only a way of taking one step forward in order to take two backward. "The way to satisfy Strom is to talk about a little poontang," said Kleindienst. "The older he gets the more he thinks of it." Once again they succeed in stalling their Southern strategist by more traditional gifts—first, a round-the-world trip to inspect the maintenance of PXs and the upkeep of military cemeteries, and then, authorization for still another infantry training center in South Carolina as a prop to the state's depressed economy. South Carolina's political payoff in new Army bases had turned the lovely land of magnolia and chitlins into the infantry training capital of the United States if not the world.

When the *New York Daily News* ran one of its friendly little chatty editorials of advice—"C'mon, Dick," it began, "how about holding a press conference and spitting in the eye of the doves, the quitters, the wardheelers, and the merchants of doom and gloom who say that you're keeping yourself under wraps for mysterious reasons?" —the White House communications boys took it seriously.

"It's not as if Dolly Schiff and Max Lerner were talking to the Bronx in the *New York Post*," said Herman Heinz, wrinkling his brow, and putting on his *Weltschmerz* expression.

"The *News* readers are *our* people," said Herbert Klein.

"Check," said H. R. Haldeman, double-checking the names of the editorial writers on the *News* in his "With Us" and "Against Us" card files.

"I've got it!" said Frank Shakespeare of the United States Information Agency. "How does this grab you: We run our own press conference, using people we can trust, and we do it in a relaxed living room atmosphere."

"Not bad," said Herbert Klein.

"Except for one thing," said H. R. Haldeman, shaking his head. "I'm afraid that in his condition Dick couldn't even sustain that. Have any of you spoken to the First Lady lately about what's been happening to him nights?"

The others kept a respectful silence. They *knew;* since none trusted even the gracious Pat Nixon, all had their own intelligence channels in the servant and Secret Service corps.

"I won't bother you with the details but it's not feasible to have Dick appear in any climate we can't control as media traffic cops."

Frank Shakespeare made a mental note of the felicitous phrase, thought for a good five seconds, and suddenly said with renewed enthusiasm: "Put this in your stomach and let it gurgle around for your gut reaction. We invent our own press conference—like we did during the campaign. Off-camera questions by one of the good, solid blue-collar voices, like that fellow who does the Alka-Seltzer spot. Then I splice in old footage from Dick's old press conferences, news speeches from the past, et cetera and so forth. It's even possible to pick up a sentence from one speech and put it with another on a master tape."

The other media men looked interested.

"Isn't there a problem about different backgrounds?" H. R. Haldeman wondered.

"I can solve that," Frank Shakespeare said, "with cut-away shots. We put Dick in a standard pose before the lectern, nodding, smiling, pointing to the next questioner, and then with the usual 'Thank you, gentlemen and ladies' at the end. When we pick up for voiceover stuff, we cut to the correspondents sitting there—they love it with the camera on them."

"He might well be able to handle it—if it isn't too much of a strain and doesn't take more than about fifteen minutes of his time," said H. R. Haldeman.

"What's he doing that's more important?" inquired Herman Heinz, a slight edge in his voice.

The others stared at him coldly.

"I mean," said Heinz, recovering, "Frank has a helluva idea here, and we don't want to throw it away by sloppy planning and execution."

The following day H. R. Haldeman killed the whole idea.

"It's too risky," he told the assembled media traffic cops at their eleven o'clock brainstorming session. "There are too many snotty bastards around from the networks and the so-called educational stations who'll want to do their stuffy analyses right afterward. Then the Democrat national committee will go into its crybaby act about

25

getting equal time to answer us. Even if it does work technically, Frank," he said to the disappointed director of the United States Information Agency, "it won't wash strategically."

Shakespeare thought for a full ten seconds and said, "What if we just distribute it to our foreign clients overseas? Then we're safe on the domestic end and get reverse feedback—from those we can trust abroad? I can play it in Greece, Spain, and Turkey for starters on video and then do a voice simulcast for the whole Voice of America on audio. Even the wise guys at the BBC wouldn't know what hit them—and they'll swallow it because they love freebees that don't cost them anything."

H. R. Haldeman shook his head slowly.

"Let me tell you fellows something, and let it sink in," he said. "I learned it from the President himself, when he was in better shape than he is now. You'll go along with me that Dick could give us cards and spades when it came to instinctive political savvy?" He waited for their nodding approval and continued. "He used to say that action will get you into trouble every time but that studied silence is the better part of wisdom for a President who represents all of the people. Dick is *entitled* to do nothing—he earned his marks when he was elected —except, of course, for the occasional appointment of a presidential commission to study a crisis and report back to him for further consideration. Now we've got a half dozen commissions going already—on riots, on campuses, on what-have-you. We can carry this stance for another half year and we'll be in for another four years."

Less than a half year before the Republican convention, the renomination of President Nixon for a third term—his hand-picked Supreme Court majority had ruled that the Constitutional limitation could be suspended in "certain overriding national emergencies"— or his eager Vice President appeared almost a certainty. Almost, but not quite, for other forces were at work in the tranquilized country.

Just when a few remaining hostile newspapers began to clamor for more visible leadership, the Administration got a lucky break. Burma, once only a little Vietnam, blew up. It distracted attention from events at home. An internal revolt broke out between the hill peoples and the so-called Kaba Makyes (Our Free Homeland), led by General Ne Win, a graduate of the Command and General Staff College in Fort Leavenworth, Kansas. The General declared martial law, jailed all rival party leaders, shut down the presses, and called for increased United States support. "Unless we back up General Win," a revived Joseph Alsop wrote gleefully, "America will lose the respect of the free world by failing to act like a Great Power." American B-52s began bombing the northern provinces.

"We are doing so strictly at the request of the free

people of Burma who are threatened by outside aggression," said Allen Drury, the White House press secretary.

At the same time, a confidential Army memorandum first printed in *Commonweal,* the liberal Catholic publication, reported that seasoned captains and majors with Asian experience had threatened to resign unless they could advance in grade following renewed American military operations; the prospect of total peace, commented *Commonweal* ironically, was demoralizing. The Department of Defense—despite the fact that it had failed to flush out sanctuaries in Cambodia, Laos, or Vietnam—drew up an ambitious plan for a helicopter assault upon Burma with a strike force of Marines and Green Berets.

In the little State Department in the basement of the White House once occupied by McGeorge Bundy—an original architect of escalation by bomb and napalm during the Johnson era and thereafter head of the Ford Foundation—his successor, Henry Kissinger, and his chairborne commandos, quickly swung into action. They immediately got on their hot lines to the Rand Corporation in California and the Hudson Institute in New York, the think tanks of high-level military justification manned by professorial social scientists, computer analysts, and retired Pentagon consultants. The answers came back on the IBM printouts: A short but well-

mounted assault upon Burma is within the realm of possibility and, all things considered, justified.

This, of course, was only a capsule of the think-tank
reports; six months later the appendixes alone—complete
with qualifications and contingencies—came to three
hundred pages, expensively bound in morocco. In a
special briefing for Spiro Agnew and an inner circle
from the National Security Council, Henry Kissinger
blinked behind his lenses and spoke:

"The United States can respond in the following ways.
One, by doing nothing at all and hoping that the Communist hill people will be satisfied with a small humiliation of our ally. Two, mounting a limited helicopter
assault to show the American presence in Southeast Asia
—though I cannot determine the domestic consequences
in an election year as well as others at this table. Three,
convening the SEATO powers in a joint package provided by carrots of military and economic assistance
plus a distracting maneuver by having a couple of carriers steam up and down their coastlines—"

"What do you gentlemen think?" Agnew inquired.

"I vote for showing the flag with the carriers first,"
said the Chief of Naval Ops.

"Chopper assault," said the Army Chief of Staff.

Agnew turned to Kissinger.

"What's your *final* opinion?"

Kissinger pulled out another set of alternatives and passed copies around the table methodically. They read the page of proposals—Kissinger had quickly discovered that the President and Vice President could never absorb more than a page.

"All right," Agnew said sharply. "Now I have six instead of three alternatives and I still don't know what you think, Henry."

"My mind is open," Kissinger replied cagily. "I'm presenting the expertise for your decision in the total mix of foreign and domestic considerations."

"Cut the cards and stop being out of character," Agnew retorted. "What do you *really* think? Our country is faced with a humiliation at home and abroad and we need answers, not evasions—and that includes from my *own* people."

"A little of each," Kissinger answered, without missing a beat. "We talk-fight. We—"

Agnew pounded the table.

"Speaking for Dick," he said, a phrase that rolled off his tongue easily, "let's not be precipitous, especially as we head toward the conventions. I would say we need more info. It's not the little yellowbellies out that way I'm worried about but those here. It's dangerous to pull off an assault this far from the nominations—and we'd be throwing away a trump card. Remember how beautifully Johnson played his Gulf of Tonkin resolution out of Congress? He had them eating from his paws right smack up against his nomination in Atlantic City."

Kissinger and his military allies from the Pentagon looked disappointed.

"But I've got the right research explanation for the public," Kissinger said. "It's a speech by President Kennedy that fits right in with the Burma situation today. You get on the three networks and begin by saying: 'The security of all of Southeast Asia will be endangered if Burma loses its neutral independence. Its own safety runs with the safety of us all. I know that every American will want his country to honor its obligations to the point that freedom and security of the free world and ourselves may be achieved.' End of quote."

"Kennedy said *that*?" Agnew said.

"He said it just that way about Laos—but it works for Burma, too," Kissinger replied. "Then you deliver your punch line—'these are the words of beloved President Kennedy and you can do no less,' et cetera."

"It's one helluva quote," Agnew said. Then he mused for a moment. "Kennedy got brownie points for the same stuff they rap us for." He turned on Kissinger. "Look, Mr. Six Options, we better not right now. But save that stuff. We may need it during the campaign if it hits the fan."

The following morning Herbert Klein himself rather than one of his button men came out of the Fishbowl

31

and announced that there would be an important statement by the President.

"Will Mr. Nixon read it—or will *you*?" asked the mischievous Nan Robertson of the *New York Times* Washington bureau.

Klein's frozen smile acknowledged the sarcasm. It was to be expected; she was from the Eastern crowd who spoke and wrote for themselves and didn't know the real voters. He began to read:

"President Nixon yesterday presided over a meeting of the National Security Council where the major topic was Southeast Asia. After consulting with his advisers, the President declared that the situation in Burma, long a trusted democracy, was of the deepest concern to the Government of the United States. Various proposals are under study and, in concert with our democratic allies in Southeast Asia, various options are being pursued on an ad hoc basis."

The cameras from the networks rolled and the newspaper pencils stood at parade rest. But nothing more followed.

"Is that *it*?" asked Marquis Childs of the *St. Louis Post-Dispatch*.

Klein nodded and smiled.

"Can we expect further enlightenment from the Vice President?" demanded Robert Sherrill of the *Nation*. "Was *he* there?"

"We never reveal the names of those present at NSC meetings," Klein said innocently.

Then he closed the press conference and retreated to the inner recesses of the headless Executive Mansion.

Nobody was minding the country.

CHAPTER 2

The Shrinking of Richie Nixon

IT HAD been going on for many months. But only two persons knew the intimate details of his "dysfunction." Pat Nixon, of course, knew only too well. The other was the celebrated Park Avenue society psychiatrist, Dr. Wolfgang Kissinger, who claimed to be a fourth or fifth cousin, once removed, of the President's foreign affairs adviser. Actually, he was no relation at all but had a highly trained public-relations flair that did him no harm professionally or socially, and in fact had become friendly with his White House namesake.

The nocturnal episodes were particularly frightening. His condition developed almost imperceptibly. At first his symptoms were mistaken for plain courtesy, and much admired. "What an extraordinary sense of noblesse oblige!" said the charmed wife of the Moroccan Ambassador, after Mr. Nixon climbed in next to his chauffeur and insisted that the diplomat and his fashionable wife ride alone on the back seat of the presidential bubbletop. Not a week later, when the President presided over a contest on the South Lawn of the White House to select the "Finger-Lickin' Chicken Queen" for the famous chain of franchise drive-ins, he signaled for limousines to take home twenty-five young Southern belles—and then stood by to open and shut twenty-five Mercury limousine doors personally.

The First Lady smelled that her husband was going through another one of his famous crises of self-confidence that she, more intimately than could be described privately or publicly, suffered with in silence. Her tight-lipped, cool stare had helped her during the worst times: when he was ridiculed by the smart alecks in the Hollywood community during his years as a Congressman and by the clever columnists and cartoonists in New York when he stood in the shadow of President Eisenhower and was ignored as an accident of political fate. And so she decided to do what had always helped to relax his tingling ganglia—take him away to one of their homesites where he strode around his wealth with a grin, telling her again what their net worth was in land and securities, and ending as usual by saying what a wonderful country it was because it had happened to them, just plain Americans.

The big house overlooking the Pacific at San Clemente was his favorite place. Good California friends had worked it out so that they quadrupled their acreage by designating it as the site of a future presidential library

to house official papers, paid for and administered by
the National Archives. He had told Pat several times
how grateful he was to President Johnson for advising
him on his post-presidential perquisites, some of which
had been written into law and some of which were
there for the asking and taking. Lyndon and Ladybird
had got their nest egg long before by free franchises
for broadcasting stations; he said that theirs should be
socked away in tangible realty holdings. Next to San
Clemente, she liked to take him for rest and recuperation
to Key Biscayne. His playful Florida neighbor and
business counselor, Bebe Rebozo, cheered him by repeating again and again how in the White House years the
value of their mutual property had doubled. Bebe
would take him fishing off Walker Cay while protective
Army helicopters hovered overhead. It was easy for the
pilots to spot their charge; he was the only one in the
yacht who fished while wearing a dark business suit
and tie.

The Nixons and their lovely daughters spent more
and more time away from the seat of anguish in Washington. The long weekends often began on Thursday
morning and stretched to the following Tuesday. "The
President is conferring with aides and has taken along
a number of reports for study and action before sub-
mitting new programs to Congress"—so went the communiqué; it would be followed weeks and months later

with a second communiqué—"The President is disappointed that his detailed programs on a number of omnibus proposals have not yet been approved by the Congress." Occasionally Mr. Nixon would be away, the public was informed, because of the holiday season. In addition to Christmas, Thanksgiving, Labor Day, Columbus Day, and other official and semiofficial holidays, he celebrated Greek Independence, Rosh Hashanah, the Feast of the Immaculate Conception, Robert E. Lee's birthday, Maundy Thursday, and the days each of the fifty states entered the Union. These would be preceded by proclamations and congratulations to the various religious, ethnic, and national organizations and their leaders. They, in turn, felt that the President was at last the President of all the people, and truly *cared*.

But the nocturnal episodes continued.

"Sit down and tell me all about it—in your own words," Dr. Wolfgang Kissinger said to Mrs. Nixon.

She had come up to New York, presumably on a shopping trip and to see old friends but actually because she was frightened by her husband's behavior.

"Every night for the past few months, whenever we're in the White House, he wakes up at two in the morning and looks around the bedroom, puzzled. He then goes to the closet, takes out his suits and shirts and underwear, and begins to pack them in an old suitcase. When I ask him what he's doing, he replies that it's time to leave. At first I looked at the appointment book, thinking that we had to be off campaigning again, but nothing was scheduled, certainly not in the middle of the night. When I told him, all he would say is, '*What are we doing here?*' And once he said, 'This looks like President Eisenhower's bedroom we're in.' When I answer that it is, he smiles knowingly, and continues packing his bag."

Dr. Kissinger pulled on his sideburns and curled them between his thumb and forefinger; he was known as a merry psychiatrist who liked to dress, act, and talk young. Unlike the talkative Henry, he was given to long paid silences.

"—and then," Mrs. Nixon continued, waiting in vain for a consoling interpretation of her husband's doings, "he actually puts on his overcoat and starts to leave. The first time it happened I was away and I heard about it through John."

"That would be the Attorney General?" Dr. Kissinger inquired.

"Yes, John and Martha are old and dear friends. John took Dick into his law firm after we lost in California when Dick's health, as you know, was frail and uncertain. Well, John was at a reception late one night honoring Edgar Hoover's fiftieth year at the FBI or maybe it was his seventy-fifth birthday, I forget which, and he tells me he got an urgent call from Dick, that is, the

President. Dick asked *him* where he was supposed to be the next morning, which client he was supposed to see. John rushed right over to the White House to see what was up. He found Dick all dressed and ready to leave for New York and the law office. John told me that it took some doing before he clarified things for Dick, gave him one of the sedatives you ordered, and put him to bed."

Dr. Kissinger said, "Good, good, and when did the next episode occur?"

"After that I decided to make sure that I never left him alone at night. Because it has become a steady occurrence—at least twice a week, and I fear it's getting worse. The reason I rushed here and interrupted your schedule is because last night, when I was indisposed briefly, Dick packed a bag and walked out of the White House front door. He told the Secret Service men following him to call a cab, that he had to make the air shuttle to New York. Luckily, they called for his helicopter instead to take him to *Air Force One*. By that time I was able to come down and call the whole thing off as a misunderstanding in scheduling."

"Did he say anything?" asked Dr. Kissinger.

Pat Nixon looked at him woefully and said, "He kept muttering that he had a client to see at Nixon, Mudge, and he didn't know what he was doing at the White House."

Dr. Kissinger broke his silence with his well-known bluntness.

"Mrs. Nixon, my impression from seeing your husband is that he suffers from a related series of incidents. When we separated the wheat from the chaff, we discovered certain things of unusual interest. He wanted to run for President again—but he was sure that he would never make it. Even if he did—he frankly told me —he was not sure in his own mind that he could measure up to the office. He kept comparing himself to Eisenhower—and wondering if he had the right to aspire to the same office. Even then, one thing about his conduct made me believe that his problem was deep-seated."

Pat Nixon looked puzzled.

"He kept holding doors for strangers, and smiling."

She nodded. "But he's always been extremely courteous," she said, defensively.

"Noblesse oblige is one thing," Dr. Kissinger continued, "but when lèse majesté is ignored and denied to an extreme, there is something seriously wrong. If one delves into the medical history of King George III, one finds—"

"*Mr.* Kissinger," she said coldly, "I am not interested in your comparisons. You are talking about the President of the United States—your President and mine."

"Mrs. Nixon," he replied in kind, "I didn't come to you, you came to me, sweetie. Why? I'm a brilliant shrink. Someone wants to know about the Soviet ABM capability, he goes to my fourth or fifth cousin, once removed, Henry, who knows more about the Kremlin's intentions than most of the Politburo. Someone wants to know what's ticking inside his head, he comes to me. Wolfgang Kissinger," he emphasized, lapsing into his professional couchside manner, "doesn't hold hands or heads—he tells it like it is."

She swallowed her pride, and said, "What is the diagnosis?"

"I can't tell *you*," the psychiatrist said, "because it is a confidential matter between doctor and patient, and, anyway, I'd better work him into the schedule for a personal visit. That will eliminate the guesswork and hearsay—"

"He definitely can't be seen coming to your office," she said. "It was different when we lived in New York and almost nobody knew. Not," she quickly added, "that there's anything to hide—lots of good Americans have a little emotional upset now and then. But he is our President, with hot lines and panic buttons, and if it ever came out that he had a little problem it wouldn't be good for the *country*."

"Then I could stop by to see him the next time I'm double-dating with Cousin Henry in Washington—unofficially."

"He has too many enemies lying in wait and checking

visitors—we have no privacy at all. The press is always ready to pounce on him. Do you know that hateful cartoonist, Herblock? The first thing you know, he'd have you carrying a little black bag labeled PSYCHIATRIST and making a house call at 1600 Pennsylvania Avenue."

"How about one of your houses—Key Biscayne, San Clemente?"

"They're there, too, with their wives and expense accounts. It's even more of a monkey cage. Let me think for a minute. . . ."

"I know the place," Dr Kissinger said. "It's where I once saw him secretly just before the last convention."

Simultaneously, they said, "Montauk—Gurney's Inn."

For several years Nixon had been using the remote beach hotel at the end of Long Island as a hideaway. And so once again they arranged a rendezvous there. Mrs. Nixon found a convenient pretext in a ribbon-cutting ceremony devised by Robert Moses, the ace highway planner responsible for more miles of concrete poured than any official in New York State history, opening another section of the Long Island Expressway parking lot. While Moses used the occasion to advance the cause of his pet project—putting a second toll bridge across the wetlands and waters of Long Island Sound for the sake of the American motorocracy he had en-nobled—Mrs. Nixon made a diversionary move upon several department stores for spring outfits. "I have

43

nothing against European designers," she said, "but I prefer our own California dressmakers." It made headlines in *Women's Wear Daily* and Suzy in the *New York Daily News* clucked her tongue, cattily offering comparisons to the former Mrs. Jacqueline Onassis's fashion internationalism.

That evening a limousine left the Moses estate on the South Shore and delivered the Nixons to MacArthur Airport for the return trip to Washington. *Air Force One* took off—but Nixon was not on it. The ruse had been successful. A second limousine sped after dark to a private beachside cottage on the grounds of Gurney's Inn where Dr. Kissinger met the President.

"It's good seeing you here, Wolfie," said Nixon.

"Likewise, Richie," said Kissinger.

They patted each other's elbows and backs and sat down to a private box dinner of cold lobster and California wine secretly prepared by the proprietor himself.

Then they began talking. The President stretched out on an Adirondack chair with his head facing toward Washington and his shoes off, relaxed. Raw instinct always made him point that way.

"Say the first thing that comes into your head," Dr. Kissinger urged his patient.

"Agrippa," the President said, his face lighting up and his eyes rolling.

"Why Agrippa?" Dr. Kissinger asked, noting the name

on his yellow pad for show; actually it was unnecessary for he was taking down every word on his hidden recorder.

"Because Marcus Agrippa defeated Antony and Cleopatra at Actium, that's why, and I always go with the winner."

"What's that got to do with the price of supported potatoes in Suffolk County?"

"You asked me to say the first name that came into my head and—"

"Give me another free association."

"Checkers."

"No, no, Richie, you're going backward—we got over *that* problem years ago."

"Nevertheless and notwithstanding, the test of great leadership is whether one has the ability, as Kipling once said, to keep his head while others are losing theirs."

"All right, cut the campaign crap and let's take it from the top again. No Agrippa, no Kipling, and no speeches."

Oblivious to what his trusted companion said, Nixon closed his eyes and continued, "One of the most trying experiences an individual can go through is the period of doubt when he is determining whether to fight the battle or fly from it. It is this period of crisis conduct that separates the leaders from the followers, the men from the boys. Did you hear me after the Burma invasion?" Wolfgang Kissinger nodded; he wondered if the President was copping credit for one of Henry's better shows. "The Presidents who fail are those who are so overcome by doubts that they either crack under the strain or—"

Nixon leaped out of the wicker chair and suddenly went to the window and stared at the ocean in front of the cottage. Kissinger walked over and put an arm around him.

"The old feeling?" he said, softly.

The President nodded. He seemed overcome.

"Don't move if you're comfortable standing," Kissinger said. "Now listen closely. Say something happy right now."

"Pension," the President said, unhesitatingly.

"Another word," Dr. Kissinger said rapidly.

"Perquisites," the President replied, grinning.

"And another!"

"Palaces!"

Dr. Kissinger frowned. "What the hell do you mean, palaces?"

"I'm sorry, Wolfie, I meant my estates in Florida and California. Excuse me."

"All right, but no games now. I want instant reactions but try using your noodle first."

Nixon nodded and tried to get a grip on himself.

"Name three points you want to make in your next message to Congress."

The President stared, blinked, and said nothing.

"What would you say are your major accomplishments in the White House?"

The President looked pained, and cast his eyes down.

"What programs do you have in mind during your third term in office?"

The President shuddered.

Dr. Kissinger shook his head. He reached for the house phone and called the proprietor. "Do you have any Dr Pepper?" The proprietor replied that Gurney's had provided the President with choice California wines but unfortunately didn't have any Dr Pepper and couldn't get a bottle at this hour of the night. "No class," Dr. Kissinger said, and hung up. He turned to the President. "Sorry, Richie, no pick-me-up."

Dr. Kissinger thereafter confined the conversation to small talk, football scores, and surfing. Once again the President smiled in recognition. His memory for professional football players was remarkable.

At dawn the Amagansett fishermen rolled their trucks across the sand and put their boats and nets into the ocean. Nixon remarked that he wished he could have a nice job like theirs. Mrs. Nixon had deliberately planted one of the President's favorite handbags in the cottage— but this time he showed no inclination to pack up and leave. It was time to return to the White House before the press and public got wise to the night out here. But Nixon wouldn't budge. Dr. Kissinger called the First

Lady on a prearranged private line and explained the predicament. She measured the degree of his panic and then told him it was all right, he would not have to go back to Washington, he could fly directly to Key Biscayne where Bebe had a private fishing party all set up for him. Only then would he leave Gurney's Inn.

In the next, and it would turn out, last, consultation between Pat Nixon and Wolfgang Kissinger, she asked him to give her the medical diagnosis straight.

"Professionally," Dr. Kissinger said, putting his Gucci loafers up on her chaise longue, "I cannot disclose the facts about a specific patient. But I can speak in general terms about a hypothetical case whom or which, for argument's sake, we will call a Richard Nixon type. The elemental facts were there from the first time he came to this office—an uncertainty about himself, a certain stiffness of manner, occasional breakouts of perspiration and a gritting of teeth, and, most surprising of all, a great desire to be not just admired but *loved*."

"Are you implying that Dick isn't loved?"

"Depends what you mean by love."

"He's a very devout person, you know, doctor, but he doesn't perform like Billy Graham."

"Nothing personal."

"Or that Dick isn't lovable?"

"Mrs. Nixon, I said no such thing. If you wish me to play back the tape—"

"What tape? Have you been recording all this? Destroy it immediately!"

"Don't get yourself so coxcited, sweetie," Dr. Kissinger said. "It's just normal routine so I can study the playback later and see if I missed anything—which is rare for me."

"Erase it then—everything I've said now and in the past—and turn that damn thing off!"

"As you wish," he replied, and reached for a switch beneath his chair. "Here," he continued, "have a swig of Dr Pepper and calm yourself." She swallowed the drink, and applied her public face again.

"As I was saying, we aren't talking about anyone we know but a certain type. Now the need of said type to be loved manifests itself in all the door-holding, the back-slapping, the campaigning in the sticks—I never heard of anyone who so loved speaking to small groups and seeing their shining faces as reflected glory. I mean, he is like, well, *uptight* for a kind word. He wants to be *cuddled* but people somehow don't put their arms around *him*. Has he ever been in an encounter group?"

"What's *that?*" asked the First Lady.

"Oh, just Gestalt therapy," Dr. Kissinger said, "derived from my late dear mentor, Dr. Frederick S. Perls of Germany. It celebrates man's freedom, uniqueness, the configuration of mind and body."

Pat Nixon looked puzzled, and bit her lip suspiciously.

"Practically, it's like getting a womb bath, or like tripping without acid. It might heighten his sensory awareness. You never know how it affects you when you drop your pants or panties, as the case may be, strip off your clothing and shed your inhibitions together with—"

"It's Communistic!"

"I might be able to get him into the one at Escondido. Hugging and kissing are allowed but no intercourse. It's very fine for the resonances, nevertheless, and keeps your hormones healthy."

The First Lady was speechless.

"Maybe you could make it a twosome." Dr. Kissinger watched the First Lady redden, her cheeks aflame. He closed his eyes and thought visibly. After a long moment he continued, "It was only a wild thought. Probably too hard to get a group together anyway for a president of the United States. We must not show our emperors without their clothes, so to speak."

Pat Nixon lowered her face in her hands.

"Let me assure you that there is nothing wrong *physically* with the hypothetical person we are discussing. Heart, lungs, bowels are all tip-top." He patted her shoulder reassuringly. "It's his *persona* that's in poor working order. As I see it, we have a case here of an individual dominated by striving toward a distant goal, in compensation for a postulated feeling of inferiority.

His drive satisfactions—the lollipop we all lick—have left a void in his development socially. The imbalance of consciousness-unconsciousness has resulted in a subordination of feeling and a quirk in life style."

"Can you put it a little more in lay language?" she asked.

"Of course. His go-go in one direction has caused a repression of what we call the personality structure, or personality, in which he has had a chronic deficiency. From the first time he visited this office and sat where you're sitting I told him that his organ dialect, as dear Dr. Adler called it, revealed exaggerated anxiety and open aggression. It would take years of deep therapy to discover the unfavorable development—which now has been exacerbated by his stay in the White House—that twisted him as an individual in his early, formative years. Attaining power has definitely worsened his condition and—"

Mrs. Nixon could no longer stand it. Dr. Kissinger actually seemed to be savoring the diagnosis of gloom as he catalogued her husband's troubles. It was any Kissinger family's trait, she imagined, but at least Henry always put his options down on paper in neat and clear one-two-three fashion.

"What is it you're trying to tell me, Dr. Kissinger?"

"I'll level with you, Patsy," he said. "Your patient and mine is suffering from one of the worst cases of rampant inferiority complex that I've ever run across in my years of practice in Darmstadt and New York."

She looked almost relieved.

"Is *that* all that's the matter? Everybody feels somewhat inadequate sitting in the White House."

"*That's* plenty, if you happen to be President. Right now he's like a submarine. If the pressure pushes him hard enough, he's liable to blow himself out of the water. He just doesn't think he's got what it takes. Perhaps he never had. *All he thinks he's capable of is running for the Presidency, not actually being the President.*"

Her mind drifted to the time when Ike had tried to talk Dick out of being his Vice President a second time. But she remained silent.

"That's the reason behind all his nightly walkouts. His behavior is queer to you and me—but it's the most honest thing in the world to him. Richie wants out, sweetie, and unless he gets out damn soon you're going to be left with what you've got now—a walking wounded."

"What can be done? What is the way out?"

"—or worse, the next stage, a total dysfunction case."

A tear fell.

Dr. Kissinger filled their glasses again.

They drank their Dr Peppers in unrecorded silence.

CHAPTER 3

The State of Spiro Agnewism

On February 12, 1976, after playing the TV road in dying Southeast Asia again, Bob Hope, "Mr. Republican Master of Ceremonies," stood up in front of the Lincoln Memorial in Washington and waved his putter. It was the signal for an outburst of spontaneous applause—cued by a dozen associate producers carrying signs that read: EVERYBODY CLAP NOW. The beloved comedian made everybody in the live audience of tourists and faithful government Republicans ordered to turn out here feel good inside. They, and later folks across the country in videoland, knew that if Bob Hope was in favor of the Academy Awards, or Abraham Lincoln, or Chrysler cars, or the Burma war, these products were warranted safe and good for American consumers.

Earlier in the morning of Bob Hope Day in Washington, the famous United States Marine Band had played a funeral medley to honor the latest casualties being reburied at Arlington from temporary graves in Rangoon and Taiwan. Now, following the familiar "From the

Halls of Montezuma to the Shores of Tripoli," the Marines struck up "Thanks for the Memory" as a tribute honoring the living Hope.

"Good evening, ladies and gentlemen," he said, though it was still the afternoon. "My Lincoln *shtick* tonight is being presented to you as a public service by Chrysler Motors, makers of fine cars, and fine human beings to represent. There will be only three commercial interruptions in the next hour because of the solemnity of this setting. Before we begin with the Ann Rutledge dancers, and my old paisan Frank Sinatra—I was speaking to Phyllis Diller the other day. You know Phyllis, that beautiful girl next door you married? Well, as Lincoln said, *If you make a bad bargain hug it all the tighter!* But no kidding, she's a real doll. We're going to send her to Burma with her fright wig to make faces at the Reds—"

Suddenly there was a flurry of movement in the audience, a group of young men and women broke out Burmese independence flags and waved them, and they were clubbed and taken away by District police. The incident was not seen on network television that night when Chrysler presented the Lincoln Memorial in glorious living color.

Now the associate producers checked the sequence of the idiot cards for the big man who was coming on next. The Ann Rutledge dancers kicked away, weaving in and out of the stately Doric columns, and then the New

Salem choir sang "Tenting on the Old Camp Ground" and "We Are Coming, Father Abraham." In a second chorus, previously filmed in a studio in Rockefeller Center, the words of the Civil War song were modified to go, "We are coming Chrysler, Dodge, and Plymouth" and the new models were rolled out in front of a blowup of the Lincoln Memorial. It was, as promised, the only middle commercial.

"Cue Agnew," whispered an assistant director into his body mike, and the obligatory wide-eyed young researcher opened a National Park Service door within the Memorial and whispered, "One minute, Mr. Vice President." A makeup girl dabbed his forehead with Kleenex, without smearing his pancake tan, and the Vice President looked at himself approvingly in her hand mirror.

On the extended wooden stage in front of the Lincoln statue, Bob Hope was reading his brief introduction. "And now, ladies and gentlemen, it is a great honor to my sponsor and myself, the Republican National Committee, and Americans everywhere around the world— including," he added with an aggressive pause, "Burma —to present *my* golf partner and *your* Vice President, Spiro Ted Agnew!"

The associate producers sprinkled in the crowd held up large signs reading: STANDING OVATION.

Atop the Memorial the reverse cameras from the National Broadcasting Company's sports department zoomed in on the audience as it rose to its feet obediently.

Spiro Ted Agnew strode forward manfully. He paused for a patriotic instant to salute the Lincoln statue. He turned and saluted the crowd out front, first to the left, then to the right, then straight ahead. People cheered him spontaneously, and laughed as the clowning master of Republican ceremonies handed him a golf club. They swung their clubs and waved them in acknowledgment. It was a neat democratic touch for the folks out there. In the master control truck, the director superimposed the face of Spiro Agnew and his putter upon Daniel Chester French's noble statue of Abraham Lincoln. They would be joined together in television history, information retrieval systems, and photo files forever—if not sooner, at the Republican National Convention in the summer. Agnew spoke:

"Fellow Americans, fellow Lincolnians, fellow Republicans. We are assembled here today to honor one of us, one of our own, Abraham Lincoln. Now a lot of people have been taking his name in vain and claiming him as an advocate of this far-out docrtine or that but, my friends, let me assure you, that man behind me was a moderate Republican, a conservative in thought and actions, and not a wild-eyed believer in permissiveness and anything goes in this Republic.

"Abraham Lincoln was a great believer in human

nature—and so am I. He did not want to shove things down people's throats—not welfare programs that would support and subsidize laziness, not schemes that would make the South the whipping boy of the North or the Eastern radical establishment, not costly plans to bus children from one community to another and set the black folks at the throats of the white, and vice versa, and certainly not the uninhibited right of the newspapers to print any and all sorts of inflammatory material that would insult the integrity of elected government officials.

"These things are all a matter of historical record, ladies and gentlemen, and Abe Lincoln said them, long before Spiro Agnew tried to bring this country back to its senses. Let me quote the sixteenth President of the United States directly. Right here in Washington, responding to a serenade in front of the White House, he said: *Human nature will not change. In any future great national trial, compared with the men of this time, we shall have as weak as strong, as silly and as wise, as bad and good.* Unquote.

"Now we are faced with new fiery trials. We have the same troublemakers at home that he called the Copperheads—those who are disloyal to their own government. In addition, we have something that he didn't have—a whole group of nations of Communist bent who are out to destroy us. They respect one thing and one thing only —strength. If they think the United States of America

57

can be bullied, can have its flag burned and spat on—at home or abroad!—then you can be damn sure that they will try a rush off-tackle or a lateral end-run somewhere, sometime, soon. That is why I say here and now, to those within the sound of my voice and to Americans the world over, thanks to the facilities of this network and my friend Bob Hope, we will not disarm, we will not pull back our commitments and our armed forces, we will stand guard on the bastions of freedom as Abraham Lincoln did for his party and country. We will not perish from this earth!"

Every schoolboy out there got the Lincoln language and felt a thrill go through the assembled civil servants and Washington tourists. Suddenly voices shouted in controlled rhythm, "Speer-oh! Speer-oh! Speer-oh! Speer-oh!" and the Marine Band on a prearranged signal struck up "Hail to the Chief." The shouts "Speer-oh! Speer-oh!" continued in the background. A gray-haired soundman in the NBC control van inquired aloud, "Have you ever heard anything like that before?" And a beat-up old radio correspondent next to him replied, "You bet your ass you have—at the Berlin Olympics in 1936, the Piazza Venezia in Rome hailing the Duce, you name it, the pee-pul are everywhere, they always applaud the lions and not the Christians, bread and circuses, pal."

The Vice President modestly pointed to the seated figure of Lincoln, as if to say the tribute was for the sixteenth and not the next President. The band segued into "Thanks for the Memory" and another Bob Hope Chrysler Hour wound up in a medley of sentiment, waving golf clubs, and the slow crawl of twelve comedy writer credits across the small screen that the Nixnew Administration loved and controlled.

By now the American public and most of the magazines and newspapers in the frightened national press had stopped asking questions about the nonappearance of President Nixon at ceremonial functions; they were getting harmless quotes and abrasive laughs from the Vice President. His habit of wrapping himself in Lincoln's words sometimes drew letters to the editor from outraged Civil War scholars and American History professors; but their corrections could barely keep pace with his utterances. It all made innocuous Sunday supplement copy, stuffed between the color comics, of the *New York Daily News* and *Parade* magazine. Seeing the pop value, *CATV Digest* invited Vice President Agnew to write a monthly feature called "Your Lincoln and Mine," which was lavishly illustrated and divided into two sections: Lincoln the Jokesmith and Lincoln's Words to Die For. The *Digest's* brightest team of senior editors began editing the "fat" out of Lincoln's language for the CATV cassette club edition.

The communications mechanics in the White House no longer kept up the pretense that Richard Nixon was running the United States from the Florida or California "White House." The usual press releases invariably included the sentence, "The President is taking a long weekend as a working vacation, during which time he will be preparing legislative programs, conferring with various members of Congress, and receiving foreign policy briefings from Dr. Henry Kissinger."

But now there was an unspoken assumption that Nixon was on the shelf, not at all well, and that somehow it was wrong to say so explicitly. At the annual meeting of the American Managing Editors Association, the top executives of a joint panel of newspapers and newsmagazines debated among themselves the role of the White House reporters. In a release issued the following week (it had taken some time to reach agreement on the semantics), the AMEA declared that their publications felt a strong sense of responsibility to the American public not to print facts that were not in the higher interests of the nation. (They could not get rid of the double negative in the compromise language.) Even if the American public did not get the message, the White House management and especially the reporters and editors in the Washington bureaus did. A few daredevil reporters and bureau chiefs who tried to file stories about the President's "dysfunction" were politely told by their managing editors that it would be—the favorite phrase of news executives—"in bad taste."

Still, the pollsters had to begin their popularity contests and line up their paid-in-advance political clients for the '76 conventions.

In his "Putzi Poll" column in the newspapers and in his weekly feed to his television clients, pollster Dominick Putzi reported that Senator Edmund Muskie was ahead of Vice President Spiro Agnew in what he called "National Acceptance." It sounded like early '72 again. The confident Putzi declared that 38 percent of the voting population of the United States preferred Muskie, 34 percent were for Agnew, and 28 percent were "undecided or unfamiliar with the jobs held in government by either Muskie, Agnew, or both." Asked by a *Chicago Sun-Times* reporter how many Americans he had interviewed to arrive at these percentages, Putzi replied that it was confidential client information he was unable to disclose for ethical reasons. "Actually," the *Sun-Times* reported, "qualified sources among his clients admit that Putzi's people interviewed 370 potential voters who were then projected to speak for some 100 million Americans."

Unembarrassed, the pollster announced in his next weekly report that for '76 he had devised a new system of interviewing for presidential elections called TIP— Total Intelligence Profile—and it would appear exclusively in his newspaper, newsmagazine, and network columns. "Election polling is a science that cannot stand still," Putzi declared, "but it is also an art. When the networks and I were partners in the '72 election, our extrapolated analysis system clearly proved that in either 42 or 68 percent of the primaries, depending on point of view of tellers and other residual factors, people voted only according to their ethnic, racial, and prejudicial predilections. But now the American voter is more sophisticated. TIP is a new system that uses a combination of computer input and information retrieval for a total profile of intelligence, based on college and junior college attendance, military service, rank attained in service, plus the normal and X factors that go toward making up a voter's mind in different regions of the nation. TIP, a Putzi Poll exclusive, is a must for accuracy because of the new eighteen-year-old voters."

To the frightened politicians in both parties, it all made sense somehow. The Putzi means were less important than the ends—a headline saying you were in the lead in the great popularity contest. To those who raised questions about the workings of the Putzi pollsters, answers were furnished by free-lancing professors from Columbia University's Graduate School of Journalism who were on the pollster's payroll and could always be counted upon to give the operation a veneer of academe. English professors, no different from teachers in the purer sciences hiring their minds to federal government defense studies, knew how to sing for their suppers—

grants, conferences abroad, and business consultant jobs —all, to be sure, in the name of the humanities.

Spiro Agnew was incensed when he watched Harry Reasoner announce the first Total Intelligence Profile result over ABC. He called together the communications *apparat* at the White House to fathom the significance of the new Putzi technique.

"What right did Reasoner have to *smirk* when he blabbered that Muskie had more so-called acceptance than I had?"

"Oh, that's how Harry delivers all his lines," Herbert Klein explained. "He's a smirker—nothing personal."

"Well, I thought I detected a little *extra* curl to his lip this time. He's getting that wise-ass David Brinkley look around his mouth. The networks still have it in for me just like they tried to shaft Dick whenever they could, right?"

The others—Haldeman, Kleindienst, Shakespeare, and Heinz—did not dispute their Acting President.

"Anyway, let's get on with it—what's the intelligence on Putzi and his people?"

Heinz wondered aloud, "Didn't he get his start doing personal polls for Joe Kennedy's sons?"

Haldeman and Kleindienst nodded.

"It figures," Agnew said. "In other words, he can be reached. He must make a pretty good buck—anybody know?"

Haldeman and Kleindienst knew—independent of each other, both had checked his most recent federal income tax returns—but they kept quiet.

Frank Shakespeare savored the moment of hesitation. He had had a hard morning—his Voice of America jamming service had accidentally knocked the British Broadcasting Corporation's overseas reports to East Europe off the air—and waited for a comforting return to domestic political intrigue.

Agnew saw it in his face. "Frank?"

"Spiro," he said, remembering his first-name training along Advertising Row, "I know Putzi from television. An operator, with intellectual pretensions. They had him polling Proctor and Gamble detergent popularity at the same time the news department had him polling the ethnics. A so-so track record, mainly remembered for the brilliance of his expense accounts." Shakespeare waited to see if the others had more information; then added, "Of course, you know why Muskie came out ahead? Because Muskie's backers hired Putzi to do independent polling for them, that's why!"

Agnew's cheeks lit up in a wide smile. Shakespeare looked pleased. They both saw the possibilities.

"I'm sure some of our columnist friends would like that little piece of information," Agnew grinned. "Who should we give it to—Buckley? Roche? Kristol?"

Herbert Klein recovered and took command.

"No, it's a little early in the game to break it. Let's just hold onto that juicy news item—which, by the way, checks out with my own sources, Frank—until we need it a little later in the game. We'll bank it for use when Muskie begins to peak."

"I suppose you're right," Agnew said. "But I'll tell you fellows honestly. I hate like hell to make the American people think even at this point that I'm not their favorite."

He had begun to believe it, and for occasional good reason. Agnew had arrived at his political station not by deceit but by mediocrity that could be trusted, and by a genuine knowledge of the ordinary. Below the bombastic tremolo was a fatalism that became his saving grace. Sometimes it would break out in humor and sometimes in anger. But never in sweat. Unlike Nixon, Agnew had no crises of conscience. His Baltimore compatriot, H. L. Mencken, had once said, "The chief business of the nation, as a nation, is the setting up of heroes, mainly bogus. No intrinsic merit—at least, none commensurate with the mob estimate—is needed. Everything American is a bit amateurish and childish, even the national gods. The most conspicuous and respected American is a man who would attract little attention in any other country. All of which may be boiled down to this: that the United States is essentially a commonwealth of third-rate men."

What neither the Menckens nor the new traducers of
the American dream recognized was that third-rate men,
powered by a religious belief in the purity of themselves,
and controlling communications, could rise to become
second-rate men by patriotic gestures, and be much
admired.

More than those who had moved their own dreams
of power closer to his, Spiro T. Agnew realized that in
the months remaining before the Republican convention
he would have to display a touch of the statesman. And
so he sought advice from Daniel P. Moynihan, Harvard
professor and Johnson-Nixon loyalist, who had brilliantly
managed to convince liberals that he was one of them
and conservatives that he, despite the Irish blarney, was
someone they could do business with.

"Don't be too surprised when I mention this name,"
Moynihan told Agnew. The former presidential counselor had met the Acting President secretly in his suite
at the Sheraton-Park after delivering a lucrative speech
before the Washington chapter of Hadassah on "The
Jewish Mystique and Our Urban Society." Moynihan
looked toward the door. "Are we talking only to one
another?"

"Don't worry about the Secret Service men," Agnew
replied. "Your privacy will be respected. You're *not* here.
Now—who's your name?"

"Lyndon Baines Johnson," Moynihan said, slowly. "The one person in our nation who now wears the statesman's toga."

Agnew swallowed, and sang aloud, "LBJ—USA." He had heard the record from *Hair*—he preferred not to remember where—and the "LBJ—USA" lyrics ran through his mind. "Kissinger briefs him once a month or so on the situation in Burma. Why should he want to see *me?*"

"Because you want to see *him*. And Lyndon's Presidential Library—his own Taj Mahal. It shows respect, it dignifies the Office of Chief Executive, and moves your campaign forward on a higher plane. It's a bipartisan gesture that the country loves. It's a touch of Americana —like your address in front of the Lincoln Memorial."

Agnew nodded and his face glowed. "Pat, you're true-blue. I want you to know that when and if *my* Inauguration Day rolls around—"

"No promises, Mr. President."

"Spiro to you, Pat."

The following afternoon *Air Force One* landed in Austin and the former President greeted Agnew personally as a surprise instead of waiting for him at the ranch. The networks and newspapers were there in full cry.

"Is Dr. Kissinger going to handle the briefing?"

"Not this time," Agnew replied pleasantly. "He has

enough to keep him busy minding the store in Burma."

"Mr. Johnson, we've heard that Senator Muskie is unhappy over your meeting here with Vice President Agnew because it signifies a lack of conviction for his Democratic candidacy. Have you a comment, Sir?"

"Yes, I have a comment," Johnson drawled, "but you fellows wouldn't believe it. Mr. Agnew didn't come all this way to talk politics and I am out of that business, in case you haven't noticed. Texas is the home of a former President of the United States and Texans are a hospitable people. It is always a pleasure to welcome folks from Washington. Now, if you fellows will excuse us, I promise to drive slowly and carefully around the ranch—at least when I have an important passenger! Y'all come back soon."

They laughed and waved and took off in the parked presidential helicopter. Half of Agnew's mission had been accomplished already; the exposure and the mood were just right. The other half was unexpected.

At the ranch they relaxed by a body count of Johnson's cattle and then got down to more serious discussions. Agnew had indeed been well briefed before the visit and reviewed the situation in the Middle East and Far East carefully.

"Honor," Johnson told him. "National honor, that's what it's all about. As long as our country doesn't skunk out, it will continue to be great and in the tradition that began in the postwar years with Harry S. Truman and with Republican presidents before and after me. How's Dick been lately?"

"Much quieter, more composed, now that he's at San Clemente," Agnew replied.

"Toughest job in the world," Johnson said. "You take all good care of yourself, hear?"

They did not talk politics, as promised. For Johnson even more than for Agnew, however, the link first to Nixon and then to his temporary successor was a political trump if he cared to use it. It meant that he could push the levers of favoritism at the Democratic convention in '76 as he had in '72. He was more interested in justifying his Vietnam record in history and screening the documents of his Administration carefully in the Ozymandian Presidential Library subsidized by the National Archives But he still had a few other fish to fry.

"Spiro," Johnson said as they flew back to *Air Force One*. "There is one little thing that has been neglected, now that you ask me."

"Yes, Mr. President?"

"Lyndon."

"Yes, Lyndon?"

Johnson grabbed his lapels.

"NASA. The space program. You know, that was my special concern under President Kennedy, and I built it up right here in Houston, caught up with the Sputniks and overtook them. It's being neglected and it shouldn't be—not just for the sake of these many fine scientists and the aerospace industries all the country over but for our honor and standing in the world. Let me leave one thought with you: If you want to ride a winner, you ride space!"

It was the wisest of bromides, delivered in all sincerity by Johnson, and it gave Agnew the lift Moynihan had instinctively guessed it would. With space, he soon got airborne.

The big givers in the major corporations and their more liberally oriented attorneys in the Wall Street firms quietly cheered Agnew when he announced that the Apollo, Mercury, manned laboratory, and space shuttle programs would all proceed at top speed simultaneously. "The peace dividend," Agnew announced, "is starting here and now. As our armed forces continue to protect the free nations of Southeast Asia against outside aggressors and the honor of the United States is upheld, America is going to be the first country to plant the Stars and Stripes on Mars. How would you feel if that planet flew the Red Star and a Soviet cosmonaut got there firstest with the mostest?"

The aerospace stocks shot up from five to ten points by the time the tickers caught up the next morning. At the Massachusetts Institute of Technology and at similar universities all over the nation, department heads began to detach task forces to prepare professorial papers for governmental grants that would feed into the revived NASA charivari. Aerospace cued a rise on the major stock exchanges. Once again the Department of Justice's antitrust division was told to look the other way when conglomerates were proposed without regard for monopoly or contiguity of interests. The most unusual linked Hughes Tool with Twentieth Century-Fox to buy up Kellogg's. When eyebrows were raised at the merger of a Texas-Las Vegas aerospace and defense and gambling operator with a patriotic film studio and maker of Corn Flakes, the law factories were called in to put it over.

The distinguished New York counsel for the conglomerate, Sullivan & Cromwell, quickly subcontracted its labors to the influential Arnold & Porter firm in Washington. In the legal argument for the merger, it was maintained that such a conglomerate was logical and necessary to advance the "knowledge industry" in the nation. "Many children will thus be able to read about America's weaponry and space ships on dry-cereal boxes while eating their Rice Krispies at breakfast," said Sullivan & Cromwell and Arnold & Porter. The antitrust division agreed. The economy began to look bullish.

Only *I. F. Stone's Weekly-in-Exile* questioned the new Agnew areospace emphasis. The headline over his sober comment from Toronto after the Vice President's announcement went: "Peace Dividend—Or Have the Martians Landed in the States?"

But Agnew had more than one string to his lunar bow. More than most men in public life, he knew that the country was divided at the polls not by their pocketbooks but by their pasts. The key was pride. The voter did not have to be made to love his neighbor; a successful candidate had to make a voter feel *superior* to his neighbor: in intelligence, in knowing what was good for the United States, in supposed inside understanding of the political process. Agnew could not articulate it but he could feel it in his raw bones. So began the monthly space shots in 1976 under the Super-Apollo manned exploration series.

The White House somehow managed to run itself while Agnew spent more and more time overseeing the moon flights at takeoffs from Cape Kennedy and landings in the South Pacific. Above all, he was responsible for the ethnic astronauts.

Joseph Francis Caltagarone piloted the command module on the Apollo 49 flight to explore the Mare Imbrium formation. As he stepped out of the scarred satellite after splashdown, the first man to shake his hand on the carrier was Spiro T. Agnew. In Washington the following week, Spiro T. Agnew was presented with the Italian Anti-Defamation League's Man of the Year Award by Frank Sinatra.

"No Polack, He" was the caption under the photograph in *Time* magazine of Walter Rankiewicz, Jr., the first man to walk on the mascon near the Mare Nectaris and return with a weighty chunk of oval-shaped rock that intrigued Apollo 50 geologists. The American people thought it was a beautiful gesture when Spiro T. Agnew invited Edmund Muskie to join him on the carrier in the South Pacific for the traditional handshake. The Polish-American press provided the rest of the newspapers with long biographies of Muskie and Rankiewicz and the hometowns of their ancestors in the old country.

"We're doing Apollo 51 for Dick," Agnew told director of communications Herbert Klein at the weekly brainstorming meeting of the media *apparat*. "I want a spick in space next."

"It's a brilliant notion, Spiro," chimed in Frank Shakespeare of USIA. "The whole Spanish-speaking world will lap it up! I'll beam it out over the Voice and get Radio Free Europe to give it up the ass to the Russkies, too. It'll one-up Castro and undermine the Chilean Reds."

Agnew beamed. "Dick loves watching the shots on TV and I know his affection for the Chicanos in California. Besides," he added, "it may give our friend Ronnie Reagan a few sleepless nights if we make brownie points with the Mex voters in his state."

White House orders to NASA headquarters in Houston threw the Apollo Mission Control into new confusion: No Spanish-speaking astronauts could be found. With only a week to go before the next shot the Nixnew team resolved the problem by discovering a washed-out Air Force flier named Jack Sanders whose great-grandfather had migrated from Mexico to Baja California. Jack Sanders received a quick restoration of retirement benefits, back pay, and promotion from lieutenant to lieutenant-colonel. He also received a new name: Jose Sanchez. As he stepped on the surface of the moon after a milk run he read from a card printed in Spanish (he couldn't understand what he was saying) and English: "In the name of all Americans of proud Mexican and Spanish ancestry I offer fraternal greetings." When the chopper carrying the spick astronaut landed on the carrier in the South Pacific, Spiro T. Agnew extended his hand to Sanders-Sanchez and, grinning, said, *"Olé!"*

Apollo 52 was beautifully executed by a team of Greek-American, Swedish-American, and German-American astronauts. Apollo 53 caused Agnew some difficulty when it was announced that the first Jewish astronaut would be at the controls of the command module. The Arab vote was insignificant in the United States so the protests by the Arab League spokesmen in Washington against "Zionist elements" in space were dismissed courteously. The real trouble came from the Jewish organizations themselves.

74

THE STATE OF SPIRO AGNEWISM

It was touched off by an article in *Commentary* which summarized a 40,000-word secret position paper by the American Jewish Committee's editorial council. The costly paper raised three possibilities: that the mission might abort and cause a wave of anti-Semitism; that, contrariwise, if the mission was *too* successful and precious metals brought back, certain hard-shelled Baptist preachers with vast radio audiences would say that "Jewish banking interests" were behind the NASA program; finally, that uninformed persons would believe that all American Jews in the Diaspora wanted to return by rocket to a supposed homeland in Israel. This last was not clearly linked except by hints that much would depend on the particular religious practices of the first Jewish astronaut.

In Williamsburg, the Chasidic sect picked up the cue and began flooding the mails and subways and car bumpers with leaflets and stickers saying: NO SABBATH ASTRONAUTS! One of their mystical leaders, the heir of the Lubavitcher rabbi, cited Scripture to prove that it would be sinful for an astronaut to take off or land on the celestial Lord's Day. A picket line was promised by the Jewish Defense League if the first Jewish astronaut was demoted from piloting the command module or forbidden to carry a Star of David in space. In Los Angeles, the leader of the Reform temple—nicknamed "Our Lady of the Cadillacs" by the Hollywood screenwriters—foresaw trouble for the nation and Californians unless a fully Americanized Jew of the Reform persuasion ("How would it look on television to have one of our own wearing a skullcap out there in the heavenly firmament?" asked the showbiz rabbi) represented his faith. The matter was finally ironed out by the Rabbinical Council and the Jewish Welfare Board; orthodox, reform and conservative chaplains from the three services were permitted to greet the astronaut (who had not been inside a temple of any sort since his bar mitzvah) as he stepped aboard the aircraft carrier for the Agnew handshake.

Astronaut Sheldon Himmelfarb had indeed landed on the Sabbath—the Houston computers had not been adjusted for the Lubavitcher rabbi's input—but the day was saved by a technicality. The carrier steamed across the International Dateline and the Sabbath became Sunday.

No such luck struck the divided black community when NASA chose a much-decorated Air Force major for Apollo 54. A spokesman for Eldridge Cleaver immediately called him "a black honkey doing the white man's work." *Ebony* magazine came through with an editorial asking for black pride and black unity. At this point Acting President Agnew, through an emissary, sent a strong message to NASA's director of operations. In effect, he said, "When I order a black astronaut at the controls, I mean a spit-shine black, not a mulatto." His

76

intelligence *apparat* had uncovered rumblings in both the redneck white community and black community, the first disliking the mulatto astronaut because he symbolized sexual integration, the second because he was overeducated, uppity, and slicked his hair in a military crewcut. Another astronaut of the right shade but inferior flying abilities was hastily substituted for what was called "backup technical reasons" and off he flew as co-pilot.

The one sour note after the successful mission was struck by the Black Panther newspaper in its headline: UNCLE TOM SHAKES HANDS WITH COUSIN SPIRO. Nevertheless, the proper message got across to millions of black voters. For when black astronaut Melvin U. Jones took off his helmet after nine days in space, he was wearing a wiry modified Afro that was right on.

After each of these electoral stunts in space, a private call of congratulations came from Lyndon Johnson to Spiro Agnew. The flattery was effective—in both directions. And it pointed toward unusual alliances and silences during the national political conventions.

In his meetings with the communications *apparat*, Agnew seemed more self-satisfied. "This is a good country with good people," he told his media advisers. "I don't particularly care who is in the White House for the next four years—whether it's Spiro Agnew or someone else from the Republican party the delegates think

77

can do better than I'm doing is just a matter of person-alities. What counts is continuing the spirit of optimism and letting the public know that this country of ours is not in the hands of the television networks and news-paper chains. If they only listened to them and their columnists and commentators, they would be totally deceived. Carping, carping, carping and sniping and picking and smirking. Pick up the editorial pages and look at those cartoonists—their black-and-white judg-ments about duly elected officials are totally and utterly immoral. I can take it and give it back in kind—I've got *my* First Amendment rights, too. But what some of them do must be judged by one criterion: Is it good for the United States? Not is it good for Agnew or the party or election."

Klein, Kleindienst, Haldeman, Shakespeare nodded gravely. Agnew had certainly grown with authority. He knew how to repeat their words as his own, and in their presence, too, a good sign of total absorption. Further-more, he knew that the news enemy had a fatal flaw: the vast distance between their pompously delivered wisdom and the plain people on the receiving end who, in their instinctive hearts, felt they were being talked down to. Agnew never made that mistake. Now he saw a chance to put one of his favorite ideas into effect.

"Why can't we do here what the United States Information Agency does overseas to bring the truth out our own way? I know all about the law, Frank, saying it's only permitted abroad—but why can't we have a Voice of America for Americans, too? Don't our own people need it as much as foreigners? I don't mean just equal time—that's reacting—but *original* time. OK, I've asked the questions—now give me the answers and, for Christ's sake, don't give me one of Kissinger's three options answers."

They thought: Agnew is even more malleable than Nixon. It was something they had been discussing among themselves for months; and they had planted the notion with him several times. Now he was spewing it back. The real question was not whether to do it but if the timing was right and the public would swallow it. Klein explained the plan for the others and, as he spelled out the details, Agnew's face brightened. When he mentioned the means of financing, Agnew chuckled aloud.

"Do you think he'll buy it?" Agnew laughed.

"He'll have to or his ass and his tax exemption will be in a sling," Shakespeare said.

The others chortled their approval.

"How soon do you think we can get it rolling?"

"Just as soon as you lift the phone and get him," Klein replied.

Agnew's call reached McGeorge Bundy at his desk at

the Foundation; he stuck close to his protected enclave. After the revelations of his bombing role in the Pentagon Papers, he had to avoid showing up at the colleges.

"McGeorge," the Acting President said, "this is Spiro Agnew. Yes, it's me, calling from near your old quarters at the White House. I sure will send Henry your regards. Now, here's the notion, and I wanted your counsel because I know you folks at the Foundation love television. It's this: we're going to start a nightly Good News Hour. Yes, you heard right, the Good News Hour—on all three networks and via the Corporation for Public Broadcasting. The idea is to let the public in on what's happening in the government agencies and in parts of the country where people aren't at each other's throats. Achievements. Rural reports, 4-H, Boy Scouts, voluntary charity, bootstrap stuff. Not the riots, not the beards, not the nightly dose of gloom and doom by the nay-sayers. They've had their say for years. Now the people ought to have a chance at the network time. One hour doesn't seem too much to ask these licensed networks. What do you think?"

Agnew pointed his finger at the receiver and nodded vigorously. He covered the mouthpiece and said, "He's mumbling the right words."

"And another thing, McGeorge," Agnew continued, "it'll give the government a chance to explain our presence in Vietnam and Burma, historically and currently.

From the time you were masterminding the show for LBJ to now. We need to educate the people to what's going on in the world the same way Radio Free Europe and the Voice of America tell those foreigners what's going on here. Yes, like truth squads in a political campaign—I had not thought of that. We follow the columnists and commentators about. With the hard facts on what's really happening. We can count on your support, then? I'll tell Dick and the right people down here that you saw it immediately. Your Foundation underwrites it fully the first year—through the Corporation for Public Broadcasting. Of course, sure, they'll go along if we tell them to, do what's right for the country. And let me say, McGeorge, your generosity and vision will get you brownie points here in Washington."

Agnew put down the receiver. He winked at the White House telecommunicators. Shakespeare grinned, "Up theirs."

So began the national Good News Hour immediately following Cronkite, Brinkley, and Smith. Surprisingly, the newspapers as well as the networks themselves loved the idea. For one thing, it took them off the hook of criticism; now it was their turn to sneer at how the combined talents of the Foundation TV department and the White House telecommunicators labored together mightily to produce another Public Broadcasting Laboratory mouse. At the same time, the Good News Hour canceled the growing number of Administration demands for speeches. The networks set down only one condition: that they be permitted to find sponsors as part of their free enterprise coda. Consequently, every evening the happy side of America as seen from the White House was presented by a bra manufacturer, an underarm deodorant, a pusher of feminine hygiene, a headache formula, and Dr Pepper.

In a typical broadcast, the Good News Hour related these stories: Volunteers in Utah trekked through deep snow to present a new stove to an eighty-two-year-old blind miner whose cabin had been ransacked by Hell's Angels; a barber gave free shaves on his day off to paraplegics at the Veterans Administration Hospital who had lost the use of their arms in the service of their country; a group of high school graduates named Julie Eisenhower honorary president of their "sew-for-dough" club which mailed socks to the boys in Southeast Asia; a candlelight procession from Silver Springs, Maryland, to the Robert Taft Memorial concluded with the presentation of the Medal of Freedom to William F. Buckley, Jr., for keeping the flame of liberty burning brightly in his column; an address by Acting President Agnew on physical fitness as the key to, as he phrased it, "working off the extra pounds and the pathological elitism of hyperactive college students who would erode the accepted institutions of our society as we know it"; and a brief documentary on the new Jefferson Davis airmail stamp contest-judging by the Daughters of the Confederacy.

After an invitation to a private White House dinner, and a confidential assignment by the Republican National Committee, Dom Putzi disclosed that the Good News Hour had resulted in 79 percent recognition and approval, 6 percent unfavorable, and 15 percent don't-knows. "Extrapolating these figures for the country as a whole," Putzi announced, "it can be concluded that the great majority of Americans desire a breather from the usual run-of-mill news about war, poverty, defense budgets, inflation, and the like. Furthermore, on the Total Intelligence Profile scale, there has been a remarkable increase of parallel percentage points measuring the popularity of Spiro T. Agnew for the presidential nomination."

Encouraged by their success on the airwaves, the White House media operatives turned to a more difficult opponent—the printed press. The needles from Izzy Stone's newsletter did not hurt because fewer and fewer people dared to read it openly. But the *New Yorker*, *Commonweal*, the *Progressive*, and a few other magazines carrying antiwar articles kept on the offensive against the Nixnews.

"The bastards behave as if they think they're running the country," Haldeman said to his colleagues. "I've got a thick skin and can take it but I hate to see the youth of our nation—the good ones—corrupted by their scummy articles. These magazines reach them in their impressionable years. The publishers ought to get their keesters reamed, grinding out all that garbage. There's only one way to let them know we mean business."

"Tax returns?" asked the Acting President.

"Better than that," Shakespeare replied. "Lawyers and accountants can always take care of tax gimmicks. No, we have to give it to them in the short hairs."

"But we can't close them down," Agnew said. "Not that they don't deserve the works for going against the best interests of the country. We have to watch our moves because the First Amendment is motherhood and apple pie. I can hear the *Washington Post* bigmouths spouting their clichés about freedom of the press. What happens after January 20, 1977, is another matter. When we make our moves—"

"Here's the pitch we've decided to throw down their alley," Shakespeare interrupted. "We hit them in their mailing rates. All aboveboard and legitimate. Under the Postal Reorganization Act, these magazine publishers have to pull their weight—if we say so. They've been getting away with murder up to now because of the very thing you mentioned, the freedom-of-the-press jazz. So you, me, and a couple hundred thousand postmen have been carrying them on our backs all this time. The figures from the new Postal Service say that fourth-class mailings cost fifty cents in manpower, not a thin dime, for every fat magazine delivered. Now if we begin to bill them for the real delivery price—"

"I see what you mean," Agnew said. "But what about our own people—the *CATV Digest, National Review?* We don't want to cut off our nose to spite our enemies."

"We can keep them in the ballpark," Shakespeare said, "by doing this selectively."

"There's another backup provision in the law we have standing by in case these magazines don't get our message now," Haldeman continued. "It's called Public Law No. 90-590. Already on the books. It prohibits mailing certain material that the Postmaster says is false and deceptive. Do you see the possibilities there?"

Agnew fingered the air obscenely.

"Beautiful, beautiful," he said. "You fellows have been doing your homework. When do we begin? Is this the right moment or do you want to hide it in your hip pocket until the conventions?"

"Let's begin right away with a series of target calls to the business side of the magazine publishers," Herbert Klein said. "The conglomerate people on top will be able to see the light fast. We avoid dealing with the editors— let them hear from *their* bosses."

85

The calls by Agnew himself were orchestrated by invitations to private dinners at the White House. They came to drink the wine of official flattery, and went away intoxicated by the right message. There were a few resignations on the editorial side when the word to cool it was passed down; but most of the major editors decided to remain and see what they could "slip through." Some of the writers rationalized by saying that if they quit they would be replaced by worse people and it was better to get something by than nothing at all. And some did not have to rationalize more than in the past; as time-servers along the assembly lines of the publishing conglomerates, with a stake in the good life, they had long since become inured to the frailties of the word business.

The English language offered many options for both cowardly and courageous writers and editors.

Imperceptibly, every new magazine issue seemed to lose a little of its valor. The readers barely noticed, any more than viewers watching the Good News Hour. For all the external forces in the country—from the campuses to the streets—reflected an unspoken despair. Eccentricity became the color of oatmeal for individuals. It was a time to run with the pack.

Even in Southeast Asia, there was an epidemic of malaise. A company of American Marines in Burma was court-martialed secretly, on orders from Acting President Agnew himself, when these words were found engraved on their Zippo lighters: "If I die bury me face down so my commander in chief can kiss my ass."

PART II

THE K. PLAN

CHAPTER 4

Box 1944

AT THIS turbulent moment in the United States two advertisements appeared simultaneously in the personals of the *Times* of London and *Il Messaggero* in Rome. Both simply read:

REUNION OF ORDER OF K. ARCHAEOLOGISTS, BOX 1944.

Ten days later two letters were forwarded to Associate Professor David A. Pringle, English Department, City University of New York, Madison Square Station, New York 10010, U.S.A.

By return mail Pringle sent round-trip airline tickets to Professor John Durham, Department of Archaeology, Kings College, University of London, and to Joseph X. Licata, c/o American Express, Rome.

Licata's British European Airways ticket took him to London on a flight that connected with Durham's trans-Atlantic flight on Lufthansa. The two men had not expected to see each other at Heathrow. A flicker of recognition passed between them; but they made no effort to move closer. When the flight was called the rather carefully tailored Durham casually got on line behind the sweatered Licata. By watching the urgent demands of others for window seats and wing seats and near-toilet seats, Durham was able to be placed, at the last minute, next to Licata. Still they did not speak. But at different times during the course of the flight both walked the aisles and studied without conspicuous attention the other passengers. Their caution went unnoticed. Their conversation seemed casual.

At Kennedy International Airport they were picked up, as both knew they would be, by Pringle. He drove them in a rented car to his apartment on Irving Place. It was only when they were by themselves that the air of intrigue cleared, their greetings came forth in punched laughter.

"Lufthansa!" Licata said. "My first time on it. You always liked to make jokes."

"I could feel it sitting next to him on the plane when the pilot walked back and asked how we were enjoying the flight," Durham said. "For a moment I thought Joe was either going to sock him or hijack his plane. Come to think of it, I've never been on one of their aircraft myself. Don't know why particularly—it was all so long ago. Still I had an uneasy thought that when we got over New York they'd let us out by opening the bomb bays instead of lowering the ramp."

"It really wasn't deliberate," Pringle laughed. "Luft-

BOX 1944

hansa was the only line that happened to come close to your Rome flight. Of course, I ruled out one line because I knew that if you saw the ticket you'd rip it up—or at least switch—and we wouldn't be sitting here together."

"Which one is that?" Durham asked.

"My old country's," Licata said. "You were right."

"Dancing in the aisles and dictators in the cockpit," Pringle said. "Not a bad slogan for their commercials. Might even serve as an attraction to some of *my* country-men."

"You can't compare your country and mine," Licata said.

"Don't be so sure. We're hand-and-glove now, asshole buddies in NATO, and things are happening here, too."

"Yes, we seem to have heard a thing or two," Durham said. "Spy-ro and all that. He's rather a dunce, isn't he?"

"He is a dunce but we're bigger ones," Pringle said. "The cap-and-bells can be dangerous on the seat of power. Don't let the tatterdemalion fool you. He's in charge, and he's ripping off many of the things you've thought were part of the permanence here. The free schools, the free papers and magazines, most of all, the free spirit. A lot of people are just plain scared—and silenced. You can smell it even if you can't always touch it."

The three men glanced at each other and broke forth in laughter again. They shared the unspoken language of an old friendship, burnished by the passing years and the realization that nothing others might find offensive could stand between them.

"But don't you have your presidential changeover on the way?" Durham asked. "I assume that Mr. Nixon is hors de combat this time."

"He's out of it, unless they pull another fast one, which is not impossible. The word reaching us is that he is finishing out his term and cashing in his chips. They have made it some sort of federal offense to print material about his health, emotional or physical, so everybody just assumes that he won't run. Agnew is more in charge now than Nixon ever was. He isn't making any wrong moves—you know about his capers in space with the ethnic astronauts. Well, obvious as it was, it gave him something Nixon never had—a man-in-the-street popularity."

Licata broke in, "I can tell you, he's even more popular in Greece. The people are very proud that someone whose ancestors came from our country is Vice President or Acting President. The Greek papers I read in Rome— under the table, as we say—have him elected the next President of the United States, no ifs, ands, or buts. And they have already extended an invitation to him to visit Athens the first time he comes to Europe as President. If the colonels had any objections to this, of course it

94

BOX 1944

would not appear in the papers. Agnew never, never raised his voice about the dictatorship in my Greece of thugs and political prisoners. A word, a phrase, a sentence—this is what the underground and the exiles hope for. But it never comes. And now you say he will become their partner for four years, eight years?"

"It depends," Pringle said, "on more than political parties and voting this time. It will depend on brave people. Of the sort we once knew so well—maybe were ourselves once. That's why I summoned—"

"David, not quite yet," Durham interrupted. "We have so few opportunities to sit upon the ground and talk of the death of kings. Of course we know you have something damn serious running around your mind, otherwise you would not have signaled Joseph and me by our Order of K. cover. I'm an old bore about those glorious, carefree days except with you two gentlemen. Besides, do you know that we in England are still not permitted to blow the cover or write anything that touches on code work? Wouldn't anyway, but still one does wish for a chance to share these things nostalgically. I cannot even raise my son's interest when I hint at devilish derring-do behind the lines in Greece and all that rot. Don't really blame him. He's seen better dramatics on BBC-2. He couldn't imagine the graybeard in his house squinting over the evening paper and marking term reports killing with a silencer. Don't know if I can myself now. Sometimes I even find myself questioning what we—"

"Balls!" Licata muttered. "The bastards are back in the saddle again. The same people, different uniforms. I don't have any regrets, only that I'm not there again with the carbine and knife, working them over. Just think of what they were and did—what they would have done in your country. Do you remember what happened at Megara?"

They had met at Megara in '44, the spring, on a midnight drop. The Germans swarmed all along the Gulf of Corinth to Athens. Pringle and Durham had trained together and jumped together, the American carrying the weapons, the Briton the radio. The pocket-size airfield at Megara had been mined with the very best from Krupp. Tortured women had informed the Germans that they were coming. But after dark, Licata and a handful of partisans had unarmed the mines and picked up the Anglo-American sergeants. Licata gave them ragged civilian clothing and drove them away in a stolen German Volkswagen. They were hidden in the hills behind Araxos. When they emerged they were "archaeologists," permitting them to travel around the countryside. Time and again, Licata saved their lives in the first few months. Then they became part of his killing team. *K* for killing; it was all so simple in those days. But they lost men, too,

BOX 1944

sometimes to Greek traitors feuding with the partisans, often to the Germans, the ferrets. But they managed to send signals out and keep the lines of communication open. By the time they paved the way for the British Red Devils striking the final blow for the liberation of Greece, the "Order of K. Archaeologists" had dwindled to three men—Licata, Pringle and Durham. Killers three.

Across the postwar years they had seen each other twice. Durham and Pringle had visited Licata in Greece ten years later, a tourist trip, seeing the islands and the places that were in German hands when they were in disguise. Professor Pringle had been there a number of times as a real archaeologist on digs; he had turned a wartime game into a profession. The three had met a second time under more dramatic circumstances: to rescue Licata from the new gunmen running Greece. Through their old codes of communication, he had managed to let them know that the colonels had isolated him as a dangerous person because of the very wartime work in the underground that had once liberated the country. Licata had escaped to Italy, with the bribe money and pressure provided by his wartime friends, and their last reunion had been in Rome.

Now they reminisced into the night and caught up on their personal lives and dreams. The British archaeologist said that the only significant change in his life in the last five years was the arrest of his son in an anti-Ameri-

97

can demonstration against their latest war. "It was one of the events that brought us closer together," Durham remarked, "because I was pinched with him. Nothing quite like being a jailbird with your own son to establish a community of feelings, you know. Otherwise, we roll along, as before."

"In a way, I'm back in business," Licata said. "We have a small organization of exiles in Italy waiting for the moment when we can do something at home. We smuggle out information and send in newsletters. I get along well with the Italians—maybe they think X. stands for Xavier instead of Xerxes. But still I wonder how many years it will be before it's safe for me to return. You know more about that than I do—will Washington just go on giving arms and money and respectability to the colonels?"

Pringle shook his head.

"I wish I could say no, but I'm afraid that I don't know. With Agnew there, expect the worst and hope for a radical change. He likes order, and the biggest sins are committed in the name of order. Anyway, I feel something working inside me that I haven't felt since we were together. I can't think of anything else. It interferes with my teaching, with my daily life. And that is why I called you together. Because what is running through my mind I cannot share with anyone except the K. team, both of you. Joe, you say you're an exile and

BOX 1944

you are—but I am an exile, too. In my own country. I wake up every morning, I dress and shave, I walk a few blocks to the city university that you can see out this window. I teach at night now because I prefer the students who work during the day and are putting themselves through on their own. Sometimes they drop off to sleep at the end of a lecture but I don't mind because they're tired after holding down a job. Most of them are wonderful young people. But I have seen my last ten years of students going off to kill and get killed in Southeast Asia. For bullshit, God, and country. And it's not going to change unless some one individual performs an act that is so startling it wakes up Washington and turns the future around."

Durham and Licata looked intently at him. They waited for him to go on. But he did not say anything further, and stared at them for a reaction. Their reaction was measured by the stillness in the room. Pringle sensed the silence.

"Agnew has to go," he said.

"A pleasant notion," Durham said, casually.

"Very difficult," Licata said, shaking his head.

"I don't know how or when or where but it has to happen. Before he becomes the President of the United States."

Durham said, "But is he really any worse than any other mumblers and bumblers and even evil men who

99

have run England and the United States and Greece in the last hundred years? Somehow all countries outlive their worst instincts and rulers."

"Do you know what it will mean to the people here if he succeeded Nixon? It'll be the real end of the American Revolution. I know I sound like a windy professor, but it's my bad training. Anyway, my case should stand on its merits, not its rhetorical manner of presentation—which I'm afraid I'm conditioned to. It will mean that this country will be dehumanized. Europeanized, if I can put it that way, because we'll be no different here than the old countries with their cunning and ancient hatred and inability to dream of change. The reason I mention our Revolution is because this is the two-hundredth-year celebration. President Spiro T. Agnew! Thank you on behalf of the Founding Fathers, my fellow Americans! I am standing here in Independence Hall, folks, and I want to thank Bop Hope, John Wayne, and the other entertainers on the program for making this a stellar day. The honored guests in our year-long national celebration will be the Gold Star mothers. I call them the Betsy Rosses of our great nation because they have not desecrated the flag of freedom. Their sons made the ultimate sacrifice so that we can long endure and walk in the footsteps of giants. Bunker Hill. Lexington and Concord. Vietnam, Cambodia, and Laos. All our bastions of freedom. Look down with favor upon us, mighty

BOX 1944

George Washington, first in war, first in peace, first in
the hearts of his countrymen. And I, Spiro T. Agnew,
can promise you no less in sacrifice, as God is my witness.
Amen, and fuck you."

Durham stood up, put down his brandy, and ap-
plauded the speech. "Well done, David," he laughed.
"If he's as eloquent as that he is sure to be reelected in
1980. That would make him President into Orwell's
1984, wouldn't it? You may have a point there. Perhaps
we can look back with a certain fondness to the rule of
George III, one of our own noble idiots. Fortunately, he
lost the war and cut us loose from *you.* Nothing personal,
old boy, but it is a dim future you outline."

Licata nodded. "What happens in the States, happens
everywhere," he said. "Washington farts and Athens
smells the stink."

"I'm talking now about myself, not about Agnew and
his junta. I'm trying to explain what I feel I must do
in *my* life. We knew what we once had to do together in
'44, and we did what we had to do without questioning.
Even with enthusiasm. For me it's part of the same war.
Remember what we used to say then? That it would take
two years to win the war and another twenty-five years
to wind up all the barbed wire and pick up the mines.
What's been working out in my mind is the historical
flow of my life. How to seize the nettle of personal sanctity and fling it back in the faces of the official bastards."

"You mean that by your getting rid of Agnew you'll be winding up the wire and unarming the mines? That's a rather singular interpretation, isn't it? To use your own word, grandiose." Durham looked troubled.

"I don't know the exact meaning of that word," Licata added, "but let's stop beating about the bush. David, what you said for your country goes for mine, too. And what you said for yourself goes for me, too. Are we talking about doing a job on Agnew or something else? Let's say what we mean plainly."

"No, listen for another minute. You have to check out my reasoning first before you hear me about what comes next. I'm talking about right and wrong and turning your back on it, rolling with the punch, giving up, leting them run the rest of your productive adult life. Between Nixon and Agnew, that could mean a dozen years! A twilight of anger, exeunt. And a silent witness to the killing, in the name of government. Do you know the craziest phrase invented by the white-collar thugs in the White House and Pentagon? *Protective reaction.* All over Southeast Asia during these years we have been bombing the villages and the homes and the people. If they have the audacity to try to defend themselves, to shoot back after we have shot at them, then our government says we are given a license to kick the shit out of them. Unless they let us fly over their heads and drop bombs on them, we will react to protect ourselves. Must

BOX 1944

we all be a part of official insanity? That's all I'm really asking you both."

"No, of course not, David, and that's precisely why my son and I were demonstrating in front of your embassy in Grosvener Square when we were arrested. I agree with you, more than I can say, because I don't know what it's like living here for someone in the academic community. We ourselves muddle along with all sorts of dunderheads. There were wars before ours that were horrible. Historically, what should some brave souls have done about the Haigs and other dismounted-in-the-head field marshals who were responsible for the deaths of millions of British and Canadian boys at Loos and Arras and places that mean nothing now? Put them up against the wall—or make them earls? That may be one of your problems in the States. There's no chance to kick someone out of office and give him a knighthood as good riddance. Richard Nixon, the Right Honorable Earl of San Clemente. Mayor Daley, Baron of the Chicago Stockades. But what do you do beyond that with the fuckups?"

"Put them on ice," David Pringle declared.

"All very well but the most any of us can do now is mark a ballot of repudiation," John Durham replied. "If we're lucky we can make a more noble gesture. Pull a Siegfried Sassoon and throw our Victoria Cross into the sea."

"But it did work for us once in the mountains north of Megara. Should we dismiss our past?"

"It was different then, David. We were officially sanctioned killers, you know, blessed by chaplains, doing it for God and country. If we killed efficiently, we were decorated. If we tossed potato mashers back at the Germans, we were recognized as friends by the Greek people. Of course all three of us would have liked to continue in that spirit but at this stage it's a game for romantics. You can't keep swimming the Hellespont forever. One reaches a peak point once in a lifetime; we had ours. The rest is coasting downhill and waving at the crowd."

"And giving in? To *them*? We used to talk of an endless web of activism. You were the one who wanted to keep the show alive—you were the Camus of our outfit." Pringle walked over to his bookshelves and picked up *The Rebel* and read the underlined words: "An act of rebellion is not, essentially, an egoistic act. Of course, it can have egoistic motives. But one can rebel equally well against lies as against oppression." Pringle looked up at his friends and said, "That's what I'm talking about —living with lies." He continued reading: "Moreover, the rebel—once he has accepted the motives and at the moment of his greatest impetus—preserves nothing in that he risks everything."

104

BOX 1944

"Then that is the point you're at," Durham said.

"Point of no return," Pringle said, smiling.

"You can count me in," Licata said. "And Camus, too."

"Risk is hardly the word for it," Durham said. "Look, let me say what the difference is. We came here to talk motives before acts. Can we, or you, do it unilaterally? We weren't acting alone during the war. We were part of a recognized, organized, even legalized, killing feast. It sounds brutal now and cynical. But we were part of something universal. We were saving, not destroying. We were not assassins."

"*They* are the assassins," Pringle replied quickly. "It's *their* legal killing feast now. In Burma—"

"And in Greece," Licata interrupted.

"And in Greece, yes, but indirectly. How do you turn off the bloodletting where we are involved, where killing is done directly in your name as an American? *By an act of faith with your ideals.* Why should only the psychotics have the privilege of execution or maiming? Look at the creatures who have crawled out of the dismal cellar of the American house in our own time. Oswald, Sirhan, Ray. The loners and losers, the brothers in death-making. They gave assassination a bad name. They were the voice of no cause. Their deeds were horrible and meaningless. The meat our stunted Caesars fed on."

"That's a long leap," Durham said. "Unless you say they represented mediocrity, which is a cause in its way. But the blame—"

"Not the blame. Rather, the sequence of events. Look at it that way, and the assassinations were fruitful. They killed the dream and dignified the underlife in this country. Stone-faced men with leaden hearts. And all very clean-cut. That is what makes them so dangerous—their ordinariness."

"No disputing that," Durham said.

"Now I come to an assassination that takes on another color. You may have read about it in the European press. It made no news in my country when it happened years back, after Kennedy and King were killed. The *New Statesman* gave the details. There was a man named Melitón Manzanas, the chief of the Spanish secret police. He was assassinated by brave men from the Basque separatist organization as a protest against the suppressions of freedom and to end his systematic beatings and electrical tortures. Here is what the Basque leader said." Pringle reached for the clipping from the British weekly and read it aloud:

"There are three reasons for an assassination. One, that the man is very dangerous. Manzanas had a memory like a computer, he knew too much about comings and goings in the Pyrenees. Two, that the man is much hated, and no one will weep for him. Manzanas was so

BOX 1944

much hated that Franco did not dare to increase the repression very much after he died. He was a great torturer, a truly evil man. Three, that there comes a moment where an assassination is historically necessary."

Professor David Pringle put down the clipping. He refilled their brandy glasses, and the three survivors of the K. Order drank together as they had done many times in the mountains of Greece when killing was much admired.

"It's a historical necessity," Pringle said softly.

CHAPTER 5

The Trojan Horse

"Spiro Agnew as a person doesn't interest me," Pringle said. "It is Agnewism that must be killed."

"Do you think that by dispatching the symbol the phenomenon will be eradicated?" asked Durham.

"Temporarily, at least. It could be a thunderclap that rouses and lingers for a while. Long enough to wake people up and start them thinking again. To see that blind acceptance is unnecessary. It's something new. Not just talk. An intellectual execution that counts. It would be something new in our time after the horrible assassinations. In a way it could be a *response* to those criminal assassinations. Put your imagination to work and try to anticipate the reaction. And even if you cannot—and I don't know precisely how the different areas of the country would react—then at least think of it practically. It would open up alternatives that are shuttered and dark now."

"I can say this," Licata added. "It would be practical

politically in my country and in other countries. The effects, I mean."

"Unless there is something worse to replace Agnew-ism," Durham said. "You have a few others waiting in the wings, do you not, who are dying to move to stage-center. Willing to kill for it. Any Enlightenment pro-duces its jackals, and oftentimes its bloodbaths. Danton and Marat—Reagan and Wallace."

"Well, I'd like to think that a revolutionary act would survive in this country," Pringle said. "It grows out of an honorable tradition."

"Unless the figure you remove is a hero," Durham said. "Where does someone like Agnew stand in the total mix of the United States? He's a cipher in England. Or a clown."

"He has a following, no getting away from it. There are thousands, if not millions, of carnivores like him all over. Let them be what they are. But put one in the White House, controlling all our lives and destinies and—"

"And, David, you now have the advantage. You haven't been flying all day, or night, or whatever it is. Anyway, your reasoning is theoretically convincing. Your logic somewhat less so, and your chances—ex-tremely remote."

Licata said confidently, "Don't worry about the

chances. It can be done. I know how to do it. It's *my* turn to pull it off for the K. team. Alone."

Pringle stood up and said, "I'm sorry. Not now, no more. You fellows have had enough of me for one long night. I was spinning even if I haven't been flying. I just had to get it off my chest and let you know why I signaled you. OK, it's time to put your jet lag to bed."

Late the next afternoon, the three middled-aged friends arose late. In the light of a new day the air seemed normal and untroubled. They walked down Irving Place to Pringle's neighborhood pub, Pete's Tavern, and stood against the curved oak railing and talked of the past that linked them. After several drinks to wash down an old-fashioned bar lunch, they wandered around Gramercy Park, continued eastward to the waterfront docks in front of Stuyvesant Town, and watched the tugboats pushing ancient boxcars against the untamed tide around the city. Licata listened to his companions talking about Manhattan's landmarks. He had been to New York only once before, to see a sister who had since died, and had traveled with her from Boston to Washington, visiting distant cousins. Now the crowds in the streets made him restless. He said he cared to see again only two places that had lingered with him—the Flatiron Building and Union Square. Licata knew their history and surprised the two professors by naming the architect of the old skyscraper and tracing him to the Chicago World's Fair. Then they sauntered toward Union Square, and listened to the brevetted park preachers selling bromides in small packages. They wound up on a bench with two nodding winos, huddled beside the golden door.

That evening at Pringle's spacious high-ceilinged apartment, Licata repeated, "It's my turn. I have the least to lose and the greatest need—greater than you, David."

"What do you mean, your turn? It's my show here."

"But you and John pulled me out of the hands of the jailkeepers in Greece. I would be behind bars now—or beaten to a pulp or dead. So this is all free time that I have left. If they caught me—"

"Hold it, hold up," Durham interrupted. "If you want to keep score on saves, I believe that I owe a few to both of you gentlemen."

"I asked you here for your expertise, not to put yourselves on the line," Pringle continued. "Let's not play the game of who owes what to whom. We never did. I've made only two or three friends in the years since we were together. It's the unnamed and unaccounted-for deeds that build something between people. And speaking of having the least to lose, if you want to use that as a test, I come out ahead. I never remarried after Ann died in the auto accident, and there's been no one important enough since. You both have families."

"Let's get on with it!" Durham said, and the three men laughed together. It was his favorite wartime phrase when things got long-winded or tight; and the partisans who were commanded by Licata learned what it meant by the intonation of his voice.

"Also," Pringle added, "prepare, scout, execute." He recalled the textbook words and so did the others. "I have only one condition—that by the time I put my plan into operation both of you will be back in England and Italy. No—don't argue or object. Because it has to be that way or I'll go it alone anyway. I'll need your ideas on the preparation, especially on getting the right weapon."

"Weapons is my work," Licata said. "It has to be a piece suitable for close use. I have a thought."

"Unless it can be done without a weapon," Durham said. "I don't know but that would be something to think about once the game plan was worked out. And that's my racket."

"Good," Pringle said. "All three of us have to be in on the plan because—"

"I have a condition, too," Durham said, breaking in. "Whatever you plan to do, there has to be a possibility of getting away with it. David, that's a must insofar as I am concerned. I don't think that I can talk you out of this but I'm not going to sign your death warrant in any plan we think of."

Pringle remained quiet. He had thought of that himself and had taken it to the point of apocalypse rather than getaway. He had deliberately avoided the final stroke in the blueprint: his own skin. He had also avoided letting himself think that behind his decision there might be a desire for personal glory. He knew that if he thought on it beyond his apocalyptic vision, the internal logic might fly apart. He was willing to take the consequences of his own deed; saving himself was a detail. Maybe a lucky break and maybe not; that could not be the test.

"Of course," he said reassuringly, after a moment.

"I can be around for three or four more days so there's little time to lose thinking of the how," Durham said. "The first thing, I would imagine, is to reconnoiter and study his comings and goings."

"I can be here for at least a week," Licata said, "and more if necessary. I didn't come empty-handed," he added. He smiled and patted the inside of his coat pocket. "I have a few things with me that can come in handy."

"Your usual bag of monkshood, mayapple, jimson weed, nightshade?" Durham inquired innocently.

"Not exactly. That stuff is dangerous nowadays. It can do more than kill you. It can get you arrested for trafficking. They're heroin-happy at the borders. You can get by with a piece but nothing that looks like powder."

"You better leave it in the apartment," Pringle said. "I

wouldn't want an accidental pickup to cause inquiries."

Licata shrugged.

"I think it would be wise for us to take a look around Washington," Durham said. "Not you, David, just Joseph and me, together and separately, as we did coming over here on the plane."

"I know the general locations which I can give you. He's got an office near the White House and an apartment at the big Sheraton hotel. I know one other important bit of information that he tries to keep secret. He owns a fancy condominium down—"

"What's that?" Licata inquired.

"Down on St. Croix in the Virgin Islands. It's an apartment with its own private entrance and all the conveniences. He rents it when he isn't there. You never know when he drops in for a weekend and the official or unofficial itinerary puts him somewhere else. But it must be sealed off like Nixon's palace at San Clemente— probably a tougher nut to crack than somewhere in Washington."

"Which is better to take from here—the train or bus?"

"The bus is always good because nobody rides it except people who can't afford better. Or you could take the air shuttle at La Guardia—it's fast and anonymous, no reservations and no names."

"There's a little homework I ought to do beforehand," Durham said. "I'll spend tomorrow at the reading room

115

of the New York Public Library—checking the newspapers for the last six months and seeing the patterns of behavior and what I can fathom about his comings and goings. Even vice presidents have to take haircuts. Things like that. Any women? Any private business dealings that take him to see his old cronies in Baltimore on the quiet?"

"I don't know the answers to those questions."

"I don't think I'll find them out either but sometimes you can pick up a hint in the gossip columns more than in the political columns. I'll give it a whirl."

"In that case I will go to Washington alone tomorrow," Licata said. "I don't want to waste time. There are a few things to see just by walking around and checking security. Our movement has a few friends in the Greek community there—"

"Better stay away from them this time."

"All right, if you think so. I can be a tourist and sign up for a sight-seeing trip. John, I'll see you the day after tomorrow. Where? You'll be around some of the places I'll be looking at—I'll find you, don't worry. We always used to."

"Not quite the same now—we don't know the terrain. But there's a place that's not too popular. The Jefferson Memorial in East Potomac Park. With its lovely words about liberty. I've always found it quieter than at the Lincoln Memorial. I'll see you there the first night."

Pringle looked at his friends. He thought: How do you build such feelings of affection in a lifetime? They have left their countries and involvements to help me. I would do the same for them; still, what links some humans and causes others to be despised? Could only the forge of war fire such feelings? Only your *own* war? And he also wondered: What am I getting them into?

He did not hear from them for three days. Going over the newspapers at the Public Library annex near the Hudson River seemed like a good way to seek clues. It was an odd place, frequented by seedy horseplayers charting the past performances of favorites before leaving to catch the daily double, and research historians clocking the records of heroes and scoundrels before rushing off to classes little concerned with the events that occurred the day before their yesterdays. He wondered if John Durham had dug out anything on the Vice President's activities. The newspapers dropped many hints but they could lead up blind—and dangerous—alleys.

He found that the magazine and feature writers repeated each other's little anecdotes, rewriting them to avoid the accusation of copying, and finally changing the point. The successive stories attempted to soften and humanize Nixon and Agnew, and the Washington columnists especially displayed a pompous calm in the wind. The government officials and the government writers assumed a stance and role-played without boldness. Both sides seemed, at times, indistinguishable. Early on, before Nixon's emotional dysfunction, the reports often included the street sounds accompanying Agnew's public appearances. There were parades of demonstrators carrying antiwar banners with the young among them chanting, "Screw you . . . Ag . . . new! . . . Screw you . . . Ag . . . new!" But in the first months of 1976 such reports disappeared from the newspaper accounts he read; with Agnew at the center of power dissenters had been detained in federal jails.

Washington had become immunized from alien sounds. The tranquility of the new order was admired by many people.

This was the main discovery made by Durham and Licata, outsiders in America, when they returned to the apartment on Irving Place after looking over the capital.

"Frankly, I haven't seen it this way since the forgotten Ike Eisenhower and the remembered Joe McCarthy were there," the London professor said. They were comparing notes after dinner at Pete's Tavern. "It's as if the Silent Generation had taken over and—"

"Or been silenced," Pringle cut in. "Most of their leaders—two of my students—have been put away." He refilled their brandy glasses and said, "Is it really all that airtight? Didn't you find any openings, Joseph?"

"It reminded me of the way they have the colonels protected," Licata replied, shaking his head. "They keep their distance—you cannot do anything to a head speaking on the television screen. They must fear the people."

"I can hardly blame them," Durham said, drily.

"I saw some opportunities for a lucky potshot from afar. And I think that if the guards could be studied more carefully perhaps there would be a way."

"Afraid not," Durham said. "The closest we came to seeing a possibility was in the Senate. We were on a Capitol tour and I asked one of the guides, quite casually, when the Vice President presided. He rarely does any longer. Too busy running things from the White House. Practically runs the show now."

The three men remained silent. Durham and Licata watched Pringle for a reaction. They sensed his disappointment; he still seemed adamant. Pringle said bitterly, "Let's get on with it!" He stared at Durham, and then lowered his eyes. "Sorry," he said.

Licata stood up and said, "I am still willing to try it if you will permit me to."

Pringle shook his head. "No, both of you have done enough. I'm disappointed but not because of anything you've done, or not done. I may be able to follow the lead about his place in the Virgin Islands." He smiled at them and said, "You see, I haven't given up the idea."

"It's that important to you?" Durham said.

"More important than anything in my life."

Durham said, "All right. Then there *is* one chance. It's obvious but it can still work. I've been thinking about it from the beginning but have hesitated till this moment."

They stared at the British archaeologist, waiting for him to explain what he had held back. And why.

"The Trojan horse," Durham declared.

"You mean the ancient Greeks?" Licata said, smiling. "Nestor, Achilles, Patroclus, Odysseus, and the wooden horse?"

"Yes, it's the only possibility. You have to work your way inside by deceit, gain their confidence, have them accept you as one of their kind. And then . . ."

David Pringle nodded.

"The method is not unfamiliar in modern times," Durham continued. "The only thing required is a scheme—a wooden horse, so to speak. They must have all sorts of people around them. Even a few from the academic community, perhaps?"

"Hardly any," Pringle said. "A few leftovers from other government departments who have been brought into the White House. A few speechwriters. But most of the college professors have avoided this crowd on principle. Most of the good ones, anyway."

"Could they find a place for you?"

"Not as an English professor—but wait a minute. You've sparked something in my mind. It's wild but so was the trick at Troy, so were some of the capers we pulled off inside the Occupation headquarters in Athens. Do you know what the Nixons and Agnews would like to have? Acceptability by the crowd they're always deriding. The Eastern liberals or radic-libs, as they put it. The seal of approval by a historian or sociologist—someone they can point to and say, 'See? we've got one on our side, too.' They've got Kissinger, of course, but he's dead on campus because of the little wars he masterminds for young people to die in. Kissinger will wind up like Rostow, at a safe school deep in the heart of Texas, unless they can shove him into a foundation, like Bundy. No, ever since Moynihan kissed Nixon on both cheeks they haven't had an official academic stooge. The question then arises, why the hell would they want me and how can I get them to think so?"

"It might work," Durham said, "if they came to *you*."

Pringle laughed. "Yes, write and say things that they love. Become a fink. Have them notice you. Right?"

"Precisely. It's a matter of making yourself visible as a turncoat. Surfacing as a public bastard. We have some little precedent for it in the British press. Suddenly some Fleet Street boyo leaves his fellow cynics in ink and becomes a defender of the established order of things—

in government, business, the arts, or whatever. The more he's denounced, the bigger following he picks up. People set their clocks on his outrages."

"I can think of several here, too. If they did it deliberately or hypocritically—"

"It doesn't matter. The end result is the same. If it works, it will happen fast—faster than you can imagine. You'll have to put up your antennae to catch their signal. The only difficulty might be in an embarrassing record. That might scare them off."

"Don't have any—unfortunately, for me. The record is one of quiet and retreat. Never been arrested, nothing but tickets for overtime parking where I couldn't understand the English in the Police Department signs. I signed the usual campus petitions and joined a few mild organizations devoted to civil rights and liberties. That, John, is what I've trying to tell you for the last few days —I haven't done enough, I haven't been involved, and I'm churning inside. I feel that I have to relate what's happening outside to me. That's where I'm at now. Why, for me, it's a historical *and* a personal necessity."

"Well, I've made the suggestion," Durham said, "and I did not want to because I think it might just work. Yes, all too easily."

"What do you mean by that?" Licata asked. "If it works it's worth a shot, isn't it?"

"Listen to me closely—both of you," Durham said,

seriously. "I've joined you here and heeded the K. summons and I would do so again. But just as you feel an urge to strike back violently, I have come around in recent years to a feeling that even the counterviolence must not be tolerated. I'm against all the killing and slaughter in the name of peace or principle. In the end the bodies on either side of an idea or government that is advanced with gunpowder become indistinguishable. The greatest number of victims are not the belligerents but the innocents. I hate your bloody wars in Asia and I despise the pious statements by your dead Cardinal Spellmans and live Billy Grahams as they bless the bombers of Lyndon Johnson and Richard Nixon in the name of the Lord. But must I take the next step and translate my hatred into animal behavior? If I do that I sink into the pit of bestiality with them. There still must be a place for old-fashioned pacifism and active nonviolent protest that separates us from them. Otherwise, we *become* them."

Durham walked over to the bookshelves. He searched through the writings of Camus until he came to an essay written for *Combat* after their war. "You were talking the first evening about the justification for an act of rebellion and the need to risk everything," Durham said. "But Camus envisioned an endless struggle between them and us, between violence and persuasion. And he wrote something that applies now."

Durham read the words from another time of resistance: "All I ask is that, in the midst of a murderous world, we agree to reflect on murder and to make a choice. After that, we can distinguish those who accept the consequences of being murderers themselves or the accomplices of murderers, and those who refuse to do so with all their force and being. Since this terrible dividing line does actually exist, it will be a gain if it be clearly marked. Over the expanse of five continents throughout the coming years an endless struggle is going to be pursued between violence and friendly persuasion, a struggle in which, granted, the former has a thousand times the chances of success than that of the latter. But I have always held that, if he who bases his hopes on human nature is a fool, he who gives up in the face of circumstances is a coward. And henceforth, the only honorable course will be to stake everything on a formidable gamble: that words are more powerful than munitions."

Licata looked at Pringle. It was obvious that he was unconvinced. "I think his words are fine," he said, "but in the meantime my country is occupied again, this time from within. The grip has to be broken—they won't permit freedom unless they're forced to. I'm sorry to have to say that what happens in Washington will tell the colonels more than anything we can do in or out of Greece."

"Joseph has said it for me about his country," Pringle said. "I admire the words, believe in them, but there comes a time for making the words count. Here, too."

"Well, I've said what I had to. I didn't think you would be convinced." Durham looked at his watch. "My return flight leaves at ten in the morning. That leaves me three or four hours of sleep so I'd better turn in."

"You could get by with much less than that in the old days," Pringle said, and they laughed together.

"Come to think of it," Durham said, after a moment, "I believe I'd like to take a last walk and look at Joseph's Flatiron Building. At night, against the sky. I want the expert here to describe the details once again. No, David, you stay and tidy up and we'll be back in no time. Come on, Joseph . . ."

When the two men were alone, circling Gramercy Park and walking to Fifth Avenue, Durham suddenly turned to Licata and said, "If he goes through with it he's dead."

Licata said nothing, staring ahead, not facing his companion.

"And you and I will have his blood on our hands."

"We went over this before," Licata said. "He knows what he's doing, the stakes."

"Give me credit for knowing them, too. I got you out here because I know David cannot be convinced to change his mind—but *you* can do something."

"I volunteered to take a potshot myself—"

"Not that, that he will not permit nor, as a point of fact, will I. I don't want to see you killed either—you know that. No, what I've been thinking about is the completion of the *symbolic* act. Just as David wanted from the beginning—killing not the person of Agnew, which is decidedly irrelevant, but the phenomenon of Agnewism. What this is all about, as I see it, is an opportunity to deflate a pompous ass, to stick it up his pride. That's the game, really—pride, face. And ridicule, the most devastating weapon you can point at a fool. You should know that from the Mediterranean."

"What do you mean? What the hell are you driving at?"

"Saving David. Giving him a plausible posture."

"And how am I supposed to do that?"

"There's a way. When you arm his piece, you put in a blank that goes off with a bang but doesn't cause any real damage."

"Balls! You do it or they do it to you. The old law applies to the colonels or the Agnews."

"But you're doing it to him, don't you see? You're telling the world you wouldn't waste a bullet on his carcass."

"How is that going to accomplish what David called us here to do? Either we're going to pull off a K. job or not. You know me, no games."

"Because," Durham continued, "it's all a game in peacetime. Part of the game is to create an image of naiveté. David is bound to be caught—no matter what's in that piece—but my way he'll at least have a chance of staying alive. We can trigger hope they won't kill him for an inept attempt."

"Are you so sure?" Licata said. "With these people?"

"No, I'm not sure. But I want to increase the odds as much as possible. If there is no slip, it will give him a chance to be captured, go through various trials and appeals. After time passes, he'll have a chance, at least, to be freed."

Durham looked into the face of his wartime companion.

"What do you say, old friend?"

"No, I promise nothing."

Licata seemed shaken; walking back, neither spoke.

At Kennedy the following day, the surviving members of the "Order of K. Archaeologists" said good-bye. Licata had decided to stay over till the next morning because he had a few preparations to make. Durham promised to see him in Rome during the summer while passing through on the way to a dig near Segesta in Sicily.

"Take care of yourself," the English professor said to the American.

"I haven't forgotten what you said," the American

professor replied. "If by any chance the Acting President doesn't get the Republican nomination, my K. plan will become academic. Right now that seems remote, as you saw in Washington."

"Will he permit a real election?"

"Who knows? They're children playing with a big toy called the United States," Pringle said. "Still, I don't think he could get away with it—this isn't South Vietnam, yet."

"Well, let's hope something miraculous happens and you abort your mission. I want to see you again—all of us."

As Durham separated from them to board his BOAC VC-10, Pringle whispered, "Thanks for the Trojan horse."

He smiled and waved. Two friends seeing a third off; nothing out of the ordinary.

Nothing that would be reconstructed later when the shock of what had happened spread around the country.

Licata spent the remainder of the day in New York buying what appeared to be harmless home-repair tools and equipment in several different hardware stores on the Lower East Side. Then he took apart an old-fashioned fountain pen that had a strong silver-plated body, detached its nib, and substituted a soft brass cap over a casing filled with powder instead of ink. He drilled a tiny hole in the back of the pen and inserted a pin. A matching bar was attached to the cover of the pen to strike the pin at its precise center.

"Waterman's," Licata said. "Nobody wants them anymore nowadays. Here's another one just like the first—I bought both for a dollar. People prefer ball-point pens because they don't need bottles of ink but I like the ones you can fill. They leave a more interesting line on the paper with more shading, more thick and thin. They're also more useful."

He showed Pringle how it worked and said, "You carry the second pen with you all the time so that it isn't unfamiliar to you or whoever sees you normally. If you pass through an electronic screen that checks metal objects for security, it's your pen. Like your money clip or keys. Then, when the time is right, you substitute the first pen—this one."

They embraced at the airport the following day.

"You haven't been here," Pringle said.

"Don't worry about me. Careful now."

"We'll meet again in Athens and look at the mountains together."

Licata winked.

"Remember everything," he said, "And good writing."

Two weeks later, Durham and Pringle exchanged letters. Neither made any reference to the fact that they had seen each other in the United States. Both hoped that they could meet soon, here or there, perhaps during the summer vacation.

At the end of his letter Durham wrote: "I was reading something by Aldous Huxley the other day about how he conceived the world in the year 2018. In it a young man who dies in the desert leaves an inscription on his house gate that ends,

> And do you like the
> human race?
> No, not much.
> THIS MEANS YOU.
> KEEP OUT."

In his reply, Pringle wrote that he recognized the sentiments, and he concluded: "I ran across something by e. e. cummings that I thought *you* might enjoy—or at least ponder. A little poem that ends,

> and what i want to know is
> how do you like your
>   blueeyed boy
> Mister Death."

CHAPTER 6

On the White House Team

THE CALL came from the White House. As David Pringle knew it would. Not from some second-team office along Constitution Avenue but from the White House itself. After the planted pieces and appearances over the past few months, he told himself that the call would come and he would answer with the proper degree of pleased surprise. It was predestined.

In the wild ramble of his imagination, his mind always took dreaming turns and then byways and forks. What, he wondered, if the condottieri around Nixon and now Agnew wore breastplates of decency? Even his favorite gossip columnist, Suzy in the *New York Daily News,* reported that Henry Kissinger had a lively sense of humor and always made humble-pie jokes. Someone like Herbert Klein had once been a newspaperman before succumbing to Nixon's irrepressible charm; newspapermen were said to have certain saving graces. For all he knew, a heart of gold beat beneath the crewcut of H. R.

Haldeman; what if he asked him to call him "Bob" and invited him to see movies at the White House? It was important, Pringle told his imaginary self, not to lose his perspective. No matter how they might be personally, the mercenaries had to be envisioned wearing their horns. Doing their real work for Spiro T. Agnew.

Time was short, and he had decided to swing for the fences the first crack. He studied the *National Review* and *CATV Digest* for hints about style and subject; he did not want to appear too outrageous but it seemed difficult not to. The *National Review* added a veneer of philosophical pretension to its venomous cracks about youth, college administrators, radicals in sex-starved communes, Washington-New York liberal journalists, and Democratic aspirants for President; *CATV Digest* mixed rugged individualism from the Harding era with Iowa barnyard humor and prescriptions for both improving love life after the age of sixty and improving the godless shortcomings of the Kremlin leaders who failed to behave in the American Way. It was an easy choice for Pringle—*CATV Digest* was inimitable but the *National Review* might be conquered by reversing his own notions and throwing in a few obfuscating phrases. He mailed it to the one name he knew, William F. Buckley, Jr., who sent him a letter of cordial congratulations to supplement the very modest payment for his article. Chairman Bill's magazine was not big with the capitalistic buck.

The breakthrough piece he titled "The Phony Advocates of Gloom," and he signed it with his title, Associate Professor at the City University. Since the old "City College" had once had a reputation for nurturing campus radicals, he knew a conservative switch from a professor would be provocative.

"In our age of indulgence," his article began, "there is a hero-villain lineup. It is one of the special afflictions of today's youth as I see them and of many adults who follow the Pied Piper songs of the immature. Too many young people divide the world into good guys and bad guys. They—and their supporters in certain newspapers and opinion magazines—are the new phony advocates of gloom as a philosophy of life and government."

Pringle had rewritten that first paragraph several times to get the right tone. He didn't want to overdo it; still it sounded like a parody to his inner ear as he put the words down. But he knew he had to overreach because his parody was their gospel.

"There is the requirement for instant gratification among the gloomsters," he went on. "The decree that infants should be fed on demand and not on schedule has been elevated to dogma up to age thirty. Now many say that patience or even prudence is not a virtue, it is a weakness; if satisfaction cannot be guaranteed right now, this minute, then the system is sick and unresponsive and needs major surgery by the White House immediately.

"I see around me another fear which I call geneaphobia, the fear of another generation. The idea is that all other groups in society are linked up in a conspiracy to frustrate the legitimate demands of youth. The other generation refuses to 'listen' or 'communicate'—which most often means, they refuse to follow suggestions.

"And then, there is the intellectual double standard that is practiced by these phony advocates of tear-down-and-destroy—which is far worse than the unfortunate but necessary search-and-destroy practiced by our gallant forces in Southeast Asia. I am referring to the tear-down-and-destroy of their own country. Let me cite a few examples of this double standard:

"Seniority and tenure are right in a university and wrong in a Congress because—despite the vast experience of so many of our senatorial committee chairmen—a university professor is regarded as a special intellectual being while a senator or congressman who is elected by ordinary mortals in a democratic way is considered suspect.

"Cyclamates should be taken off the market because we do not have proof that they are harmless, and marijuana should be legalized because we do not have proof that it is harmful. That is known as logical reasoning.

"General Motors, Ford, and Chrysler should be attacked by the Ralph Naders as enemies of the Republic because they are unsafe, polluters, and big corporations while the University of California's rebels at Berkeley, the brick throwers and bombers at George Washington University, and the radicalizing law professors at Yale who teach their students to challenge instead of respect the courts are supposed to be cheered and, what is worse, subsidized with federal funds."

Once the dialectic got rolling, Pringle found he could invent it endlessly. There was a formula to the lunacy, he saw: Keep it simple, keep on the attack, don't examine the reasoning and the language too closely, and hit-and-run. He had to keep reminding himself to avoid statistical support for any assertions he made that appeared vulnerable on their face. Toward the end of the article he thought it would be wise to take a chance and subtly—subtly!—compliment the Acting President. He had little time to put the K. Plan into effect and he knew he had to go for broke.

"Mr. Agnew is regarded by many of my colleagues in the academic profession as the antithesis of what used to be known as an egghead. And yet it would be difficult for them to disagree with his ideas if, somehow, they originated from another source. If one reads his points closely, one finds that it is Agnew who is on the side of learning, freedom, and justice for the many instead of the disruptive handful who presume to speak for the majority. He is in favor of the traditions held sacred by his great ancestors, Plato and Aristotle, the respect between teacher and student, the right to excel by use of mind and hand instead of lumping everybody together in a neo-Freudian adjustment in the classroom, the discipline of rigid thinking instead of the loose talk that followed permissiveness. If one of the heroes of the counterculture said these things, he would be saluted as a defender of freedom of thought but if Spiro T. Agnew says it—in his own way—somehow it is deemed anti-intellectual! Who is real? Who is a phony advocate of gloom about his own, his native land?"

The Buckley bush telegraph operated rapidly. The dearth of minds in the conservative movement made those in it lean upon each other for comfort. Scores of letters congratulated him for his courage and sincerity. In one letter forwarded from the *National Review* there was a plastic Madonna and a request that he bless it. Another, marked personal, contained what seemed to be a strong hint that he join the letter writer, a lady in New Orleans, in a trip for which she would foot the bills. He turned down four invitations to speak to veterans groups and debate members of the Lexington Democratic Club, none of which would bring new attention to his reverence for the Acting President. But he did accept the chance to speak to a combined luncheon of the International Rescue Committee and Freedom House under the chairmanship of Leo Cherne. Although Cherne did most of the talking and hustling for funds for his organizations, Pringle did manage to repeat substantially what he had written in the *National Review*. Several members of the old Vietnam lobby were on hand, brought to life by the leadership in the White House, and seeking new worlds to conquer in Burma under the guise of rescuing patriots from the grip of bloody communism. When he was asked to join the board of a Cherne committee called "Friends of Burma," he thought he might as well hang for a sheep as a lamb and signed up.

But what finally brought him to the attention of those he hoped to reach was a reprint of his *National Review* piece in *TV Guide*, the most popular publication of all. The *Guide* editors changed his title to "The Happiness Quotient" and promoted it as the uplift article that week. While it contained the same lunacy as before, they had added a touch of instant psychoanalysis—a question-and-answer test for readers to decide if they were "happy" or "gloomy" about themselves and their country. A week after the article ran there came an invitation to meet the editor, a Nixon-Agnew confidant; he decided not to overplay his hand and cooled his supposed ardor. Apparently he scored with the Administration's editorial scout. The next important phone call reacting to the *TV Guide* piece came from the White House.

Had someone calling himself an "appointments secretary" set up luncheon with Acting President Agnew a few months before, Pringle would have hung up on one of his clowning colleagues. Or if by a wild accident he had been selected to lunch with Agnew in the past, he would have turned it down as a matter of principle and to avoid apologizing to his friends and himself. But it was foreshadowed and planned now, and he had to move the lunch—assuming it was for real; he still permitted himself a small doubt—to the next plateau in the plan.

Agnew was indeed for real but the lunch itself was not. It was on a small table in front of a couch in the Oval Room. He was given a choice of yogurt—prune, apricot, vanilla, or plain. "I never eat much at lunch," Agnew said, "but you go ahead and eat whatever you want." Pringle settled for apricot yogurt as the closest to food but the White House was fresh out, and he found himself talking and dribbling vanilla. With the coffee came a hearty choice of desserts—apples or oranges.

"I sure appreciated reading your gloomster article in *TV Guide*," Agnew said. "We're having a hard time with the profesors—every President but Kennedy found them yapping at his heels and you could have some of his. I personally don't give a second thought to them but some people in the country take them seriously. I feel being attacked by one of the profs is like being bitten by a caged parakeet. Nothing. My colleagues take them seriously but they're sensitive and I've learned to take it and dish it out, too. How'd you make out on the happiness quotient test?"

"A little better than average," Pringle replied.

"I scored damn near perfect," Agnew grinned. "Well, I don't expect the man who made up the questions and answers to do well on them or it would be cheating."

Pringle let that one go by; he doubted if the publisher himself knew that his editors had recast the article to build up the self-help angle.

"What you said fit in with one of my favorite projects," Agnew continued.

"I know, sir," Pringle said. "The Good News Hour. Was that your concept?"

"Absolutely," Agnew said with a touch of pride. "I got sick and tired of hearing all the prophets of gloom—"

"If I may say so," Pringle interrupted, "then it was your idea in the first place that put me on course. That program fixed my mind and made me rethink many old concepts that I lived with on campus. It inspired me to write the article, and I am glad to admit it frankly to you as originator."

Agnew smiled and got up to change his shirt. He

changed three or four times a day because he had a mortal dread of germs. While buttoning his shirt and zipping his fly, he talked about the strong need to explain all that his administration was doing in the next few months, and even afterward, depending.

"Depending whether the American people see it my way," Agnew said. "And that brings me down to the nitty-gritty. I've looked into your career. It's clean as hell. You're well respected in academic circles, I am told, and you had a patriotic war record. I need someone like you around here to work on some of the position papers and also to show the professors that not everyone is against Agnew. As a professor-in-residence who will look broadly at some of the ideas we're working on in the field of communications. Will you come aboard?"

He thought for a moment about some of the disastrous academics who had put their theories to work in the State and Defense Departments and played games with young lives in Asia. But wasn't that the reason behind why he was in this incredible game in the first place?

"I'd consider it an honor—if I could make a contribution," he replied, thinking of how Gary Cooper pawed the ground with his feet when he delivered lines like that.

"Welcome aboard!" Agnew grinned.

Disengaging from the university was surprisingly

easy; a leave was arranged and one of the school administrators let it be known that having someone on "the other side" could be useful. But it was more puzzling to his colleagues. They had kept still when his article was published, believing that it was simply another example of the need to find an outlet for professorial papers. "Publish or perish," and all that. Behind Pringle's back they sneered.

The English Department went through the motions of a farewell lunch. He found himself mouthing phrases about the need to keep openminded and objective. Responding to their polite silence, he made a few feeble efforts to justify his leave and wondered if he could deceive them, too.

What hurt was the headline in the student newspaper: PRINGLE TAKES A POWDER, JOINS AGNEW COLLEGE OF CARDS. The story quoted at length from the *TV Guide* reprint and added, quite inaccurately, that White House aides were good for at least $35,000 a year. "You can hardly blame the good and quiet prof for trying to make a buck for himself," the school paper concluded. Actually, he was receiving a modest per diem and some expenses which added up to less than his pay as a professor. He played it out to his last week on campus, writing a letter to the school editor saying that he was on leave for reasons of principle and to learn about the workings of government from the inside, not to increase his salary. It was the kind of statement that would be read in the right places for his purposes.

He was assigned a small office, modestly furnished in standard government-gray steel, but discovered that the White House credentials were magical. The perquisites included Mercury limousines with chauffeurs to take him anywhere. The pool of secretaries and the duplicating machines did not require begging and apologizing. Even the memorandum pads simply saying "The White House" carried force. Pringle said to himself, What if you were from the academic sticks and learned to love the prestige? How would that really determine your decisions and excuse the failings of the Administration that sustained you in such style?

He stuck to his knitting at first, letting them use *him*. He showed up at the receptions when they needed someone from "the academic community" and he became their "professor" on the scene. Occasionally he was asked to contribute to a staff paper prepared by one of the agencies for Agnew. His dealings with Agnew himself were at a distance—until he got his first break and was invited to an informal meeting of the communications *apparat*.

"Welcome aboard!" said Herbert Klein.

"Welcome aboard!" said Frank Shakespeare.

"Welcome aboard!" said H. R. Haldeman.

"Welcome aboard!" said Herman Heinz.

"Welcome aboard!" said Richard Kleindienst.

Not all at the same time; separately and personally. They made him feel at home; they looked like such nice people. He wondered if they had all been Navy men. But no, even the secretaries at the White House, come to think of it, had piped him aboard as he was introduced. He felt as if he was drifting out to sea. It was the way they talked topside.

"We thought you could make a special contribution to our communications effort," Agnew said, slapping him on the back and smiling. "I've talked it over with these gentlemen and they're all familiar with your wonderful articles. We want to buck up a few spots where we're all hard at work. The first one is something I take a little credit for—the Good News Hour. We want to keep the momentum and interest alive between now and the campaign. The second one is Frank's show over at the USIA, but only if you find the time. There aren't any votes overseas so it's a different ballgame there. It's the pinpricks that we have to endure from our beloved allies who enjoy needling us. We have to do something about that. Any ideas, Frank?"

"Try this for starters," Shakespeare said quickly. "We have Davie Pringle organize a cultural conference with overtones and undertones of a literary nature. That way we can grab the best names by the nuts. The overall aim is to get our hooks into the eighteen-year-old voters through the medium of their respect for printed writers—"

"They respect writers? I don't think they read them unless they have to," Agnew said. "I myself don't have the time to read anything but the newspapers and watch the networks. We don't want to be the instrument reminding them that they haven't done their homework, Frank. What do you think, Bob?"

"It might work if David rounded up our kind of people," Haldeman replied. "The most serious creators but with popularity. Top people like our own Allen Drury and Sidney Hook—people we can trust."

Herman Heinz shook his head.

"I have a nagging instinct against it," he said. "Remember that White House Festival on the Arts during the Johnson Occupation?" Agnew nodded. "It was a disaster," Heinz continued. "All the Lefties with their petitions and wiseass speeches right on the lawn here—"

"We could handle them over at Justice," Kleindienst said. "Nothing says they have to be invited. If they cause problems on the outside, we cordon off for a thousand yards all around. I happen to be looking into two of those people now. They say the craziest things and it's hard to know if they're kidding or serious but they present no problems to me."

Agnew turned to Pringle.

"It could work," he said, "but you'll be running a risk because Herman's right, they aren't rabid fans of the Administration. And I can only toss it back to you on this one because, much as I admire Drury and Hook as true American writers and thinkers, they're what the kids on campus call bad pizza. It's a risk."

"I think we'd better settle for a dinner at the White House instead of a bang-up affair," Agnew said. "We'll have them in for a USIA advisory commission night. David can help on the invitation list."

"I'll check with you later on it, Davie," Frank Shakespeare said. "If we get the right people with forums, it could break a few balls in the right places."

"My main interest is still the Good News Hour," Agnew said. "First, is it having a proper turnaround effect on the people in the country? Are people feeling better about their leaders in Washington? Second, how is it being used to further the cause of the political campaign? Are we pushing the networks and papers in the right direction so that we can get at least an even break?"

"We can check it through by polling," Frank Shakespeare said. "I'll get Dom Putzi to do one for us privately."

"Not Putzi," Haldeman interrupted. "He'll only give us what he thinks we want to hear."

"Then get someone we can trust," Agnew said. "What

about Foundation underwriting for a second year? Are we covered financially?"

"Mac Bundy and his television boys will do what we want them to do," Frank Shakespeare said. "All they ask is that it go through the Corporation for Public Broadcasting or they might get in trouble with Internal Revenue and lose their tax exemption."

"We know a little about that subject, don't we?" Agnew laughed. The rest of the media men laughed, too. Pringle did not know exactly why but he felt that he had to join in the inside joke, too. They mentioned the millions of dollars that the Foundation had poured into television vanity ventures.

"Let's get down to the substance of the shows," Agnew continued. "One thing that needs improving badly—the physical fitness part. You gentlemen remember that on one of the first programs I got on the air and emphasized the need for working off excess pathological energy by hyperactive college students. Isn't that an area David can give us some guidance on?"

Pringle rarely watched the Good News Hour, and he hoped they didn't quiz him about it.

"I'll be glad to help out," he said. "Intramural sports is something I've always believed in." He thought that would go over well.

"No, Dick emphasized sports and that was his image," Agnew said. "Mine is something more practical and concerns every living American, jock or not. Keeping fit and daily exercise—that's my image. Now how can we push that on the air so we can get the message across better?"

"You might make a few more talks on the subject," Haldeman advised. "We might be able to have you do a two-minute feature on physical fitness every evening."

"With audience participation," Frank Shakespeare added.

"No, it's too private and I don't want to stress that openly. I don't mind if it's called the Spiro T. Agnew Physical Fitness Program for All Americans, or something snappier. It'll actually make people feel better, help their circulation and constipation, and whoever does that picks up friends by the millions."

"I've got it!" Frank Shakespeare said. "We get a broad with big tits in a tank suit throwing her muscles around and rolling around a set built like a bedroom or living room."

"That's one of your better ideas, Frank," Agnew grinned.

"It could be appealing with the right actress," Herman Heinz said. "One of ours, someone like Martha Raye or—"

"Not Martha Raye," Agnew said positively. "She's a great gal and has done a lot for our boys in Asia but, let's face it, she's been over too many hills for the image we want to project."

"Someone like Ginger Rogers or Rosalind Russell," Herman Heinz said.

"Maybe one of the Miss Americas would be better," Frank Shakespeare said. "After all, it's the youth vote we're after."

"You said it for me, Frank," H. R. Haldeman agreed.

"Let's make sure she's a Republican," Agnew said, "and that she's never posed for *Playboy*."

"I know the Miss America people very well," Herman Heinz said.

"Maybe David can handle her properly—give her some lines to say," Agnew grinned. "You gentlemen stay away—I'm assigning her to David personally for coaching."

They laughed and winked.

Miss Marybeth Caserta of Canton, Ohio, was tracked down at the Sands in Las Vegas where she was doing a strip act with a trained myna that seized her bra and G-string in its beak and tugged when goosed in the tail feathers. Heinz had her flown to a small cottage owned by the Interior Department on St. John's Island in the Virgins for a check-out before going on national television. He and Pringle flew down in an Air Force fighter for the interview and rehearsal.

"I never really made it to the finals," Miss Caserta, a ravising brunette standing six feet in high heels, said. "I've heard that the girl from my state who did was playing around with two judges from the Chamber of Commerce and American Legion. Anyway, she married one of the old farts later. I didn't give a shit about winning, anyway, just wanted to take my act to Vegas. So I cooled it and smiled till my teeth ached and won the 'Miss Congeniality' title and now I'm making five bills a week and picking up another two or three big ones whenever I feel like free-lancing. My agent tells me you've got a network show that could be my big break."

The culturally minded Heinz said, "You may or may not make it because we have three or four other girls we're considering but we'll be glad to see you do your stuff." Actually no one else had been found in the Miss America lists of the last three or four years who had registered Republican and measured up to the right physical proportions but Heinz decided to hedge when Miss Caserta opened her mouth. "We understand that you're a registered and committed Republican."

"Yeh," Miss Caserta replied, snapping her gum, "but don't hold that against me—the Canton Chamber of Commerce said we had to. I don't have to make speeches, do I?"

"Not at all," Heinz said quickly. "We need someone for a physical fitness spot on the Good News Hour—the Spiro T. Agnew Physical Fitness Program."

"I like Spiro," Miss Caserta said. "Whenever he talks he says something with balls."

Pringle and Heinz exchanged glances. She was a lively one, all right. Heinz had brought along an exercise book used by the Air Force, and Miss Caserta went through her paces. There was no question about it: she knew how to shift her body into high gear and it would be hard to tune her out. She was signed up with a warning and a name change.

"Miss Caserta," Heinz said, "from now on you're Marybeth Case—we're dropping the last three letters in your name because it's more American and less ethnic this way and we don't want it known that you used to shed your garments at Las Vegas. And one more thing. Would you wash your mouth out with soap, please?"

"For a grand a week less ten percent," the former Miss Caserta said, "you've got yourself a deal but don't tell me how to talk, Hermie baby."

Heinz swallowed and agreed; after all, a nonprofit foundation was putting up the money.

"And extra if I have to deliver any lines," she added, baring her teeth.

Marybeth Case did pick up an extra three hundred for her regular appearances. The communications *apparat* heartily approved the line that Pringle wrote for her to open and close her nightly series of chesty push-ups: "*Exercise* your right to vote."

The Acting President himself congratulated Pringle for the phrase addressed to the young voters of America by the former Miss Congeniality from Canton and myna stripper from Vegas. Frank Shakespeare struck off prints from the Good News Hour showing the stacked physical fitness champion in her tank suit and distributed them to the outposts of the world as a service of the United States Information Agency to combat communism.

Wandering around the White House to become more familiar with its layout, David Pringle encountered Henry Kissinger. They had been introduced but Pringle had never been invited to see any of the papers of the bargain-basement Secretary of State.

"How's it going in Burma?" he inquired.

"Beautifully," Kissinger said. "We're winning the hearts of the populace in three different ways. Way one, through the presence of our advisory force that is sharpening up their fighting force; way two, through an infusion of American cultural historians and sociologists from our leading universities who are teaching the Burmese to recognize and preserve their ancient artifacts and traditions; and way three, by the introduction of our consumer goods and appliances which they're crazy about. How's by you on the Good News Hour?"

"It's very popular," Pringle said. "We've got a sixty percent share of the nighttime viewing audience which only proves that Mr. Agnew was right—people want to see the good side of this country, not the deep-voiced prophets of gloom on the regular networks."

Kissinger suddenly edged closer and whispered, "Good side is right—especially Marybeth Case. Is she your girl friend?"

Pringle answered, "Well, no."

"Because I'd like a knockdown," Kissinger said.

"Sorry," Pringle said, "but she's got a boy friend who she's shacked up with—the basketball coach of her old high school in Canton."

Kissinger drew back in mock indignation. "I didn't mean anything like that, believe me. I had three reasons for meeting her, none of which were sexual. Reason one, I wanted to check her Midwestern reactions to some of the domestic considerations involved in our Burmese program; reason two, because—"

"You don't have to give me all the reasons," Pringle interrupted. "By the way, give my regards to your cousin, who I knew around New York."

"Wolfgang's not really related—just a little game we play," Kissinger said. "A friend of the Nixons."

"How is Mr. Nixon these days?" Pringle said, casually.

"Don't ask," Kissinger replied. "Better to let sleeping presidents lie."

"Let's see each other—we're both from the academic world, after all," Pringle said.

"Oh, that's all behind me," Kissinger said indignantly. "This is the real world here, not the world of theoretics. Here my staff and I are putting all our knowledge to work realpolitikally. I don't have to sit around classes with a bunch of dirty snotnoses anymore." He hesitated and then stared hard at Pringle behind his owlish glasses. "You sure she's shacked up with someone else or are you saving her for yourself only?"

"I wouldn't kid you," Pringle said.

What hurt Pringle were the frequent needles he received from his colleagues at the City University. In the *New Republic* and *Commonweal* he read articles which deliberately went out of their way to jab him for being an instrument of the Nixnew Administration. "Certain cultural-educational commissars in the White House are living with delusions that they can influence the course of events but academic sellouts only serve as window-dressing for politicians," went a piece by a former friend in the English Department. When he tried to call one of his colleagues, and then another, he found a wall of silence at the other end of the line.

Still he had to keep up the pretense: to follow the K. Plan to its conclusion. And he made sure that the criticism of him was conveyed to the circle of loyal aides around Agnew. For if their enemies in the universities hated him, he became one of them.

They praised him in the communications conferences where every decision now pointed toward the convention and election. His opening came when Agnew invited him to contribute to one of his speeches. Although the

153

palace guard was omnipresent and the Secret Service men always nearby—even if hovering discreetly in doorways—he began to find himself able to enter the Oval Room where Agnew held court in Nixon's chair without being announced. The Acting President loved to invent dictionary words and phrases to improve himself and impress the vocabularies of the American electorate. Pringle succeeded in slipping in a few that Agnew incorporated in his speeches: "hysterical hypochondriacs of history," "positive polarization," and "pusillanimous pussyfooters."

If he could continue to contribute phrases that Agnew lapped up as catnip for his vanity, his opportunity to strike would come.

It would depend on what happened at the Republican convention. Maybe by some miracle Agnew would not get the nomination. Maybe the Democrats would nominate someone of principle who would not have to receive the imprimatur of Lyndon Johnson and the party wheelhorses; in his temple complete with five hundred thousand personal photographs near the banks of the Perdernales, Johnson scowled across the country at any candidates who failed to pay lip service to his greatness. And there was always the chance that even if he was defeated in the election, Agnew and the Attorney General would not allow anyone else to be sworn in.

Pringle kept up the pretense. He took to wearing a

jeweled American flag in his lapel. The bumper sticker on his car read: *America—Love It Or Leave It.* By now he had lost all of his old friends and colleagues. Still he dared not write to Durham in London or Licata in Rome —for their sakes, in the event that he had to carry out the K. Plan.

He thought: the only way Agnew could survive was to lose the election.

PART III

THE BODY COUNT

CHAPTER 7

Conventions and Election

THE AMERICAN people, who had practically nothing to say about it, were faced with an unusual choice in the 1976 presidential election. In some ways it was a reprise of 1972.

The Republican ticket was Spiro T. Agnew for President and David Eisenhower for Vice President.

The Democratic ticket was Hubert H. Humphrey for President and John Connally for Vice President.

The two most influential persons behind the scenes never appeared at the conventions nor were they present in smoke-filled rooms nearby. But they pulled long strings in the national committees and among the handful of party functionaries who dictated the nominations. One was the beloved Mamie Eisenhower, widow of the General who had served his country faithfully in war and peace, and the other was Lyndon Johnson, who briefly sounded out the possibility of a last hurrah for himself, was discouraged from doing so, and threw his support behind the only proxies he could trust.

The first problem for the Agnew forces was to disengage gracefully from the notion that Nixon somehow was still the President of the United States. More than one president in the past had become hors de combat while in office but none had ever wanted to continue running while not functioning. Nixon was an exception. Despite Dr. Wolfgang Kissinger's diagnosis, Nixon's campaigning instincts came alive a few weeks before the Republican convention. His wife had tried to keep him secluded at San Clemente but somehow he had communicated with Agnew and summoned the Acting President. As a courtesy, Agnew had answered the call and appeared, thinking it might be a propitious moment for announcing that Nixon had formally ruled out a third term.

"I have something a little hard to say, Spiro," Nixon said, when they were alone, except for Pat, "but you know I've always thought the world of you, right?"

"Right, Mr. President," Agnew said, not paying close attention.

"I picked you as my running mate in '68 and '72 and you built a name and the chance to make a personal fortune, right?"

"Right, Mr. President."

"Well, Spiro, it's a different ball game in '76."

"You can say that again, Mr. President."

"This time I'll need a second man who can run off-tackle while I carry the ball over the line."

Agnew looked up, puzzled.

"So I am leaning toward Ronnie Reagan for Vice President and I hope that you will be the man who will personally nominate him at the convention."

Agnew exchanged glances with Mrs. Nixon. She shook her head and put her finger on her lips as if to silence Agnew.

"Well, Mr. President," Agnew said, still not getting the message, "I would think that the choice would be mine just as it once was yours. I would rather pick my own Vice President."

"*You* would rather do what?"

"I said that with all due respect I want my own man—and I've decided it's going to be John Connally."

"Your man—Connally? I don't know what you're talking about but if Connally is anyone's man he's Lyndon's."

"But you made him your Secretary of the Treasury."

"And a lot good that did me or the economy, Spiro."

Agnew shook his head, puzzled, and again pleaded with his eyes at Pat Nixon.

She turned to him and said, "Would you mind leaving Dick and me alone for a few moments?"

When Agnew left the room, Mrs. Nixon turned to her husband, saying, "Dick, remember? Your promise to me and Wolfgang? We've got everything we ever wanted?

We married off the girls to rich boys, we've got Biscayne
Bay and San Clemente, we've got the investments Bebe
Rebozo made for us."

"That's right," Nixon said, his eyes glazing, and as if
by rote, repeated, "Biscayne Bay, San Clemente, Bebe's
investments for us."

"So you won't have to run for President again, remember? Just as we decided."

"That's right," he repeated, "I won't have to run
again."

"So will you tell Spiro that you've decided to let him
have his chance now?"

Nixon suddenly snapped awake. "Agnew is a Vice
President, he's not presidential caliber!"

"That's what they used to say about you, too, Dick.
Remember what Ike tried to do? He didn't want you a
second time, did he? But you showed him."

"But what about the country, Pat? Can Agnew be
trusted with it?"

"With the right people around him, yes. And with
the right Vice President to succeed him—just as you and
I planned it."

"Now I remember," Nixon said. "Just as you and I
planned it. I forgot myself for the moment, thought it
was time to run again, answering the old fire bell in the
night. Do you think you can put it over? Will Spiro and
the convention take our choice?"

"He'd better—they'd better," she replied, pursing her lips. "Or else—"

She summoned Agnew. Nixon stepped forward to greet him again. This time he shook his hand and said, "Spiro, you're my first choice for President, and I'm going to do everything possible within my power to support you."

"That's more like it, Mr. President," he said, smiling toward Pat. "Now there are a few details to handle before I leave here today. First, we'll need a statement from you saying that you have decided not to run again."

"But what reason shall I give?"

"Don't worry about that. We've got it all worked out for you. The staff drew up this little statement which I'm sure you'll find sets the right tone. Your staff—Klein, Haldeman, Kleindienst and the rest of your close friends. Let me show it to you—"

"Don't bother," Nixon said. "Just let Pat check it."

Perspiration broke out on his forehead. He looked slightly green. His hands shook as he rose from an easy chair and left the room without saying good-bye.

Pat Nixon had already seen a draft of the release without Agnew's knowledge. Her lines into the White House were still strong despite her husband's absence for over a half-year.

Agnew read aloud: "After eight years in the White House and more than three decades of service to my country, I have decided not to run for a third term, even though the Constitution and our Court says I can. In a difficult and all-consuming job, I have done my best. It is now time to pass the baton and move up younger men. I do so not for my sake but for the sake of the United States. I recommend to convention delegates that they select as my successor my loyal and efficient Vice President, Spiro T. Agnew."

He looked up at her for a reaction.

"It's passable," she said. "But it needs a few little corrections. Cut out that phrase 'all-consuming'—it's too personal."

"Certainly," Agnew said.

"And then there's the question of the last sentence where Dick picks you to run for President."

"What's wrong with that? I've paid my dues. I've stuck to Dick through all this difficult period. Besides, that's the way they drafted it."

"Well, it's negotiable at the very least," Pat said firmly.

"OK," Agnew said, "what's the price of Dick's endorsement in the release and convention?"

"The vice presidential selection," Pat said.

Agnew's eyes narrowed. He looked like a wounded chipmunk surprised by a hunter. Or huntress.

"Who's your name?"

"A young man who'll help you by capturing the new youth vote."

"Who's your name?" he repeated, baring his anger.
"David Eisenhower."

Agnew threw back his head and laughed aloud.

"Dick and I have been in this business a long time," she said. "It's our business, you know. We're talking about more than ten million new voters."

Agnew shouted, "But it's illegal! You have to be at least thirty-five years old to be eligible for Vice President."

"That's the rule for President. But we have checked this out very carefully with Constitutional authorities and the age of the Vice President is not specified. At the very least, it's ambiguous. David would not be running for President."

"But what if something happened to me? The Vice President wouldn't be able to succeed me."

"Under the laws of succession both before and after the recent changes, he certainly could. The Federalist Papers, the Constitution, the Chief Justice, and Dick's own Associate Justices who would interpret it as well as the Attorney General are all on our side."

"You mean you've checked it out that far without first consulting me?"

"They owe their places in public office to Dick, you know. The same, by the way, as you do."

"How the hell old is David, anyway?"

"He'll be almost thirty by the time of your—and his—

inauguration in 1977. That's a legal age for a Representative so it's not too unusual. And you know that under certain circumstances the Speaker of the House could be eligible to succeed to the White House."

"The Republican party wouldn't buy it!" Agnew said, desperately.

"Don't worry about the party. They'll do what's right for the country. After all, David is President Eisenhower's grandson. And the party knows that Ike ended twenty years of treason, as Dick used to say, and restored Republicans to office."

"He may be Ike's grandson but more to the point, he's your son-in-law, and the public will yell nepotism."

"Not to David—and Julie. Can you imagine them campaigning? It will restore the country's faith in our young people."

Agnew looked at her and saw the Pat Nixon he always suspected behind the mask. She was a real antagonist— but he held the high cards.

"This is a matter which the convention ought to decide," Agnew said. "There are many factors at work— Ronnie Reagan wants my place on the ticket and the convention may decide to let him have the Vice Presidency. Then there's Governor Wallace, who can be the spoiler. He ruined the Democrats by running in '72. I'm willing to trade with him for Cabinet places—just as

Dick did with Strom Thurmond—but if he makes a run for it this time he'll be stealing my votes more than the Democrats. That's why John Connally makes sense and why he could be the one to short-stop Wallace in the South. With him on the ticket spelling fiscal responsibility plus Southern responsibility, we'd be a sure thing and be able to continue what Dick would have accomplished if—"

"If nothing!" Pat Nixon declared. "The way to carry on Dick's Presidency is through David Eisenhower—and that's final!"

"Final?" Agnew said. "Says who?"

"You'll see at dinner," she said. "Will you share a Dr Pepper?"

Mamie Eisenhower had been well briefed and in her straightforward way told Agnew that she agreed with *him* that David would make an ideal running mate. She had come forward from the guest wing at San Clemente at the last moment and Agnew knew that he had been trapped.

"Ike would have loved the idea," she said, innocently, "and I think it was wonderful of you to think of David."

Agnew mumbled that it certainly was a provocative notion.

"Otherwise," Mamie Eisenhower said casually, "I was leaning toward Governor Reagan—when I thought that neither you nor Dick were seeking the Presidency."

"I never regarded you as a political person," Agnew said to the former First Lady.

"I'm not but I'm learning fast," she said, smiling.

When Agnew returned to Washington he discovered that the communications *apparat* knew all about the deal.

"Mamie's our trump card," Frank Shakespeare said with enthusiasm. "Pat says she's willing to go out there and pull a Rose Kennedy for her grandson. It's one helluva ticket."

"We don't just want to win," Richard Kleindienst said. "We want to win big this time."

"The television crews are doing a documentary about David and Julie already," Herbert Klein said. "They're going to tour every campus from Massachusetts to California in advance of the convention. We've got our people in the delegations primed for the nomination. Wherever we've gone and sounded out the ticket they've loved it."

"But what about Reagan? He's not going to sit still for it—and he's liable to make the first move against *me*, not the vice presidential candidate."

"We've added it up by the numbers," Klein said. "You've got it. But it has to be part of the package."

"With young Howdy Doody?" Agnew said, sarcastically.

"He's our boy," Shakespeare said. "Howdy Doody and Julie may not be a grabber to you, Spiro, but think of winning with a ten-million-vote margin. The Democrats are too dumb to put up someone who'll appeal to the eighteen-year-old vote. We've got to think of our ratings, our polls, and our numbers. He may not be the smartest kid to come down the pike but he's American all the way. I can see him raising his hands in the old Ike V-for-Victory sign and making young and old love him for it."

"One thing we have to do, gentlemen," Herbert Klein said. "Even among ourselves we'd better stop calling David Howdy Doody. It's the kind of nickname that can hurt. We're talking about a young man who can carry our side forward to '80 and even '84. He can grow in office. He believes in this country which is more than can be said for the troublemakers his age. If we start thinking of him in new terms, we'll convince ourselves as well about the Eisenhower-Agnew team."

"The Agnew-Eisenhower team," Frank Shakespeare said.

Agnew swallowed and nodded.

At the convention in L.A., as expected, Ronald Reagan made his move first. But he represented the past. The communications *apparat* made sure that a packet of still pictures of him as a boy cowboy, boy detective, boy lover, and boy soldier and sailor was put in the hands of every delegate. Playing up his movie past, they succeeded in reminding the delegates that Reagan was an actor instead of a Governor.

The Rockefeller forces fared poorly because the word was passed that he would build more Albany malls and would bankrupt the country with programs to help "foreigners" in South America, Africa and Asia, and people on welfare in the big cities in the United States. Rockefeller did not help his cause when he made a speech, as head of the New York delegation, implying that the resigned President had not bombed enough in Burma.

"If I am chosen by my fellow Republicans here in lovely L.A.," Rockefeller said, "I promise that governments will not be sold down the river to the Communists in the name of an easy way out. My record in foreign affairs is long and clear—I have always supported Presidents when they fought to uphold the name and honor of this country and I have opposed Presidents who have tried to withdraw American interests from the far corners of the world."

To the very end Mayor Lindsay dreamed of getting the call from the Democrats, or independent Republicans. The Agnew communicators with straight faces slapped him for switching with a trick: they ran an old film of Lindsay seconding the nomination of Spiro Agnew for Vice President, long ago at the 1968 convention in Miami Beach. "The sons-of-bitches," said

Richard Aurelio, the Mayor's political agent, in a remark that was translated by the *New York Daily News* to read, "Dick Aurelio loudly said that the Agnew people who replayed Hizzoner's seconding speech were off-springs of female dogs." The delegates would have turned down Lindsay in any case because his Republican money had dried up; later he failed to get the Democratic bid because of his anti-Burma war stance.

The seconding speech for Agnew as President was made by none other than Strom Thurmond. "He is the greatest Vice President since John C. Calhoun," the South Carolina Senator said, "and I am honored to put my faith in him for the highest office in the land." He followed Bob Hope, a California delegate to the convention, who abandoned his old friend Reagan and nominated his new friend and golfing partner for President.

Spiro T. Agnew himself put David Eisenhower's name in nomination for Vice President. "In the Second World War," he began, "I served under a man who led the Allied armies to victory. That same man you nominated to be President of the United States. His name is sacred in Republican annals in our century. He was a winner all the way! I refer to our own Dwight D. Eisenhower!" The delegates cheered and marched for fifteen minutes—as if Ike was on the ticket. "The young man I am about to nominate bears that same name," he continued. Some of the uninformed delegates looked startled but they were reassured by the party elders. "I first met him on the lawn of the White House, playing ball with his college classmates. Like his sacred grandfather, he was interested in sports and physical fitness for all Americans. He believes in a sound mind in a sound body. As you all know, he wanted to be a member of the Washington Senators and devote his life to professional baseball—and, my fellow Republicans, the Senators could have used him! Instead, he turned to his family and to the Republican National Committee for counsel. At my urging, he decided to devote his life to service to his country—like his grandfather and like his father-in-law, Richard Nixon." Again the delegates cheered the name of the abandoned President as if he were running again. "And now it is a great honor to nominate for your Vice President and mine, David Eisenhower!"

The delegates made the right noises and broke out the Agnew-Eisenhower banners. David Eisenhower was escorted to the platform by Mamie, Pat, and Julie, and as he lifted his hands in a double V-for-Victory, Spiro T. Agnew grinned slyly.

The Democrats as usual were divided at their convention in Miami Beach again. It was almost a replay of '72. The primaries had only served to emphasize the divisions. At his ranch in Texas, Lyndon B. Johnson smacked his lips and kept his silence as he read the results from New Hampshire and Wisconsin. The mixture of Eastern liberals and Western populists, Chicago big-city operatives and Southern conservatives led to confusion and a drain on preconvention funds from the moneyed opportunists who were on all sides. When the figures from the primaries emerged, McGovern, Muskie, Lindsay, and Kennedy canceled each other out. Lindsay and Kennedy immediately issued statements that their names had been entered without authorization (though both hastily added that they were grateful for the confidence placed in them by voters). Only the enigmatic Eugene McCarthy actually insisted that his name be taken off the ballot in the primaries. "I don't have to play in the minor leagues in '76," he declared. "There's no special reason for me to keep proving myself again and again. If the Democratic party wants me, they know where I can be reached." And he went off to Castine on Penobscot Bay in Maine to complete a volume of sonnets.

Senator George McGovern, who showed growing strength early in the campaign, irritated the party pros by continuing to talk about the need to get out of Burma and exorcise the "ghost of Vietnam" and confess to national wrongdoing. "If I want to confess," said Mayor Daley of Chicago, "I can always go to church." George Meany of the AFL-CIO said, "I don't need a dove to tell me what's good for my millions of trade union members and my country." Actually, what hurt McGovern most

173

were the sympathetic pundits in the press who kept repeating that he lacked "charisma" and would be talking in the wilderness while Agnew was talking to the peanut gallery. They generally agreed with what he said but doubted if the voters had the capacity to listen to him seriously.

Strangely, it was McGovern who gave Muskie "religion" and pushed him to the left, hurting his chances for a broad consensus. After the publication of the unofficial Johnson Papers in 1975 by the *Texas Observer*, linking him to Nixon's Administration as a behind-the-scenes adviser, Muskie began talking out on his own. With McGovern pressing Muskie to denounce Johnson and those around him and Muskie finally doing so in his calm but effective manner, the party regulars were in a state of despair by the time they arrived in Florida. The Left was occupied by McGovern, the Center once considered Muskie's was now unoccupied, and the Right was held by Scoop Jackson representing the defense industry interests.

Then the hidden hand of Lyndon B. Johnson became visible. At the very moment that the delegates assembled in Miami Beach, Johnson invited George Wallace to his ranch. "It's purely a personal visit between two Southerners," Johnson told reporters. "The Governor of the sovereign State of Alabama desires to set up archives and a library and we think we have the know-how here that can be useful to others who are historically minded." And then he winked.

The word was quickly passed to the key delegations at the convention that Governor Wallace would stay out of the race as a third-party spoiler if—. If John Connally led the Democratic ticket. Not only would he receive the support of Wallace but Johnson himself would go out and campaign for his Texas protégé. The second man on the ticket was said to be negotiable; this was considered a bid to some favorite sons from the larger states to get on the bandwagon.

It was at this point that the hesitant Eugene McCarthy dropped his trochees and appeared at the convention. "There will indeed be a third-party candidate in this election if the choice is between Agnew and Connally," he announced. "I will enter as an independent. For the first time in election history a deal is on between the Republicans and Democrats to nominate two candidates who have the seal of approval of past presidents who have been repudiated. And furthermore," he said, referring to David Eisenhower, "the first attempt at a Children's Crusade actually led by a child."

The party elders and bosses flew back and forth between Florida and the LBJ ranch and a deal was worked out to block the troublesome McCarthy. Connally was given second place on the ticket and Hubert H. Humphrey was named the "healing" candidate for President.

"LBJ is my leader," the exuberant Humphrey declared in his acceptance speech. "When the chips are down and the votes are in we will pick up the Great Society goals of health, civil rights, social progress and prosperity, and opportunity for all Americans."

The Humphrey-Connally ticket presented McCarthy with a dilemma. Instead of coming out against his former colleague from Minnesota, he decided to remain silent but encouraged voters to write in his name as a token protest. Even he recognized that the Agnew-Eisenhower alternative was too much to contemplate.

On Election Day, millions of voters stayed away. "The only vote that counts is the vote that is not cast," said an editorial in the *St. Louis Post-Dispatch,* and many disgusted people in both parties felt the same way.

The sound of Humphrey and Connally grated; their politics of joy carried a false ring. The young voters did indeed prove to be the margin of victory. They refused to take the lesser of two evils, preferring the apocalypse.

On January 20, 1977, unless something unheard-of happened, Spiro T. Agnew would become the next President of the United States.

Strangely, the secret introduction of ten thousand more American "advisers" into the rebellious hills of Burma was only a minor factor in the campaign. Few Americans were told that there was a real war on. It was like old times.

CHAPTER 8

President-elect Agnew

"FOR THE first time in the history of the American Republic," wrote I. F. Stone in his exiled weekly, "the Vice President, the Acting President, and the President-elect are the same person. With the clearest mandate since Lyndon Johnson beat Barry Goldwater, there is no stopping Spiro T. Agnew. The only chance is by impeachment and that prospect is, if anything, even more fearful. For his successor, the Eisenhower boy, would be made into chopped meat by Congress—not to mention Moscow and Peking. It looks like a long night for the people of the United States below this Canadian border. The only hope is that the next four years will turn into an interregnum where nothing happens to cause the President to make a serious decision—especially in the international arena. The thought of Agnew on the other end of the hot line making instant responses to Moscow's hard-liners is enough to scare the wits out of the world."

Still the initial announcement by President-elect

Agnew did have a tone of stability. "As my first appointment it is a great honor for me to report that J. Edgar Hoover has agreed to continue as Director of the Federal Bureau of Investigation, indefinitely." It was good, in a dreadful way, to know that he was not rocking the boat immediately.

Nor did David Eisenhower show that he was feeling his oats too soon. He and Julie were given ceremonial assignments but Agnew held onto the space program for himself. He had gained his popularity through the ethnic astronauts and decided to keep the Apollo take-offs and greetings on national television in his own pocket. Pat Nixon tested him by requesting that the space shows be transferred to her son-in-law, but Agnew reminded her that she was now speaking to the President-elect who would run things himself. She swallowed, and returned to San Clemente. In the meantime David Eisenhower was pleased to receive lessons from the Southern committee chairmen to prepare him for his role as presiding officer of the United States Senate. He had only one favor to ask the President-elect.

"Well, what is it? The senators say you haven't turned in your last two homework assignments."

"It's not that, sir, and I promise to complete my new lessons. This is something I've dreamed about ever since Election Day—and I've been practicing every day for the last month."

The President-elect looked suspicious.

"What I want to request is, May I throw out the first football of the season for the Washington Redskins?"

"Sure, David," the President-elect told the Vice President-elect, patting him on his close-cropped head.

"Gee whiz!" the Vice President-elect exclaimed. "Wait till Julie hears about it! Thanks a million!"

Now Agnew began to take the steps that those who feared his ignorance and pride expected of him.

"Things are going to be a little different around here," he told the communications *apparat* at their weekly session. "When Dick was around—no offense, gentlemen —there was a certain looseness in relation to the branches of government and to outside quasi-government institutions, such as the press and television. Would you agree with that?"

"Well, Dick had his style of operating," Herbert Klein said, "and you are entitled to have yours."

"I can tell you that Dick was planning to crack down on the divisive elements in the country before his unfortunate condition developed," said Richard Kleindienst·

"Right, Spiro," Frank Shakespeare said, ambiguously. "There could undoubtedly be a tightening-up all the way down the line. What's needed is the right game plan."

"Precisely," Agnew said, "and once again I'll need your good counsel. You remember what happened when the Pentagon Papers spilled all over the newspapers? The betrayal of our country's secrets? The undermining of national confidence in our country's leaders? The self-appointed journalists who went after a scoop regardless of our national interests? You know that all happened when Dick wasn't on the alert. Do you follow me so far?"

The telecommunicators nodded in unison.

"Well, that shit is going to cease," Agnew declared. "Whether it's by Executive Order, new statutes in the United States Code, or a damn Constitutional revision, nobody is going to open up their files about the internal workings of the Agnew Administration, is that clear?"

Once again their heads wagged in agreement.

"The same goes in spades for the private media who break the law and reveal secrets to our or my enemies. Now here is what's going to happen," Agnew ordered. "I want a Commission on the Bill of Rights to study the ways to update the first ten Amendments in light of changes in America. This country started out as an agricultural nation with one united group of people. It's a new ballgame now. You have central cities and regions, suburbs and warring states that have to be pulled together under a new federal system. As I see it, the big stumbling block to change is the First Amendment. The press gets on its high horse every time a program is set out by the Administration and picks it to

180

pieces. There is no opportunity for the federal government to put across its ideas fairly. You have the Cronkites and Brinkleys and their little bastards in Washington ripping you to shreds. And as I've said before, you've got the smirkers and sly analysts in the *Washington Post, New York Times, Boston Globe,* and the rest of them filling their columns because they're given space every day. The broadcasters we can control through the Federal Communications Commission. I want calls to go out inviting the heads of the three networks for a session with this group—and I am willing to attend for a little while. It would be below my dignity and a sign of weakness to negotiate with them personally. Then I want the same session held with the top ten papers, regionally speaking, but with their publishers only. Keep the editors and columnists out of this—they'll sing for their suppers and do what they're told to do, believe me."

"We've already been in touch with both the broadcasters and publishers," Herbert Klein said. "They've agreed to add their own nightly Good News Hours to their schedules."

"In prime time?" Agnew inquired.

"Right before and after the regular evening news—we'll bracket them," Klein said.

"Good going," Agnew said. "And what about the publishers?"

"They were waiting for the outcome of the election," Frank Shakespeare said. "The usual stall to see which way the wind was blowing. Now they know. Our game plan is to have them all add one full page or space equal to their editorial page for official federal government announcements. It's now in negotiation but some are making noises against anything that sounds official. They're citing the First Amendment and—"

"That's precisely what I'm talking about," Agnew said. "Why I want a Bill of Rights Commission created. I want it all to be absolutely legal and in order."

"We were doing all right by hitting them in their mailing rates," H. R. Haldeman pointed out. "They got the message. You notice that they cooled it during the campaign and stopped the name-calling and ridicule."

"Not enough," Agnew replied. "We can't just depend on moral suasion because they'll still slip in stuff and we can't police thousands of papers without hiring a huge staff and losing our own tight control. I'd rather follow up in the interim with Public Law 90-590. Prohibiting use of the mails for material the Postmaster says is false and deceptive. But I want the long-range Commission. Any suggestions for members?"

"John Wayne and Gene Autry," Frank Shakespeare proposed.

"Good," Agnew said, "but we'll have to clear them with Ronnie Reagan—they're his people."

"What about Ronnie himself?" Herman Heinz suggested.

"OK, but as an ordinary member, not as chairman—we don't want him taking it over."

"Since we're dealing with the First Amendment, wouldn't it make sense to have some people from the print media? I'm thinking of Rolf Minton of *CATV Digest* and J. Willard Marriott of the motel chain," Richard Kleindienst said.

"Willy Marriott is with us all the way," Agnew said, "but how do you figure him as a press person?"

"They put out a motel magazine for clients and staff," Kleindienst explained. "It's read by millions of people. Willy writes a monthly column that makes many of the necessary points. The pursuit-of-happiness angle."

"I'd rather keep him in reserve for other jobs—maybe in Commerce or the Federal Reserve System," Agnew said. "But let's go ahead with Rolf Minton. I'd like to see him take on the chairmanship. He's got the clout and circulation."

"Would you want him to take the top spot over Bill Buckley?" Frank Shakespeare wondered. "Bill is our most articulate spokesman on the USIA advisory commission."

"He's got enough on his plate right now," Agnew said. "I'd rather keep some of our best people on the outside as independent supporters. But there are some others we need to give the Commission credentials. Someone who is respected by everybody, someone like Milton Eisenhower."

"He's not on our side," Richard Kleindienst said.

"Not even with David Eisenhower as my Vice President?"

"Especially," Kleindienst said. "Milton is the maverick brother. I tried to enlist him in order to build up support in academic circles and he told me off but good. If he didn't carry the Eisenhower name, I would have retaliated."

"The hell with him, then," Agnew said. "All right, let's wrap it up with the addition of our most respected members of the professional bar—Chief Justice Burger and John Mitchell."

"Do you think Burger will buy it?" Heinz wondered. "There might be a conflict of interest."

"No sweat. You've read his excellent dissents on the publication of government documents. I've already spoken to him about it in case you well-informed fellows haven't heard. He sees the wisdom behind prior restraint of dangerously antigovernment material. No yelling 'fire!' in a crowded theater and no yelling 'fire!' in a democratic country—it's the same legal theory but the newspapers haven't learned their lesson yet. In fact, Burger wants to go up and down the line of the ten Amendments—and so does John Mitchell—and filter out what is no longer relevant or doesn't work. The basic language can be kept with a few minor inserts to put across the idea. For instance, 'reasonable' search and seizure. Trial by jury 'where capital crimes are involved,' and the addition of 'preventive detention' in the public interest. There's a lot of stuff that hobbles the courts and effective government which we're going to update. In the new spirit of '76, while we're celebrating the two hundredth anniversary of this country, the Agnew Administration will modernize the glorious work of our Founding Fathers."

H. R. Haldeman punctuated the President-elect's remarks with an approving, "beautiful, beautiful." Agnew grinned his pleasure. "The Bill of Rights Revision Commission will need careful handling," Haldeman added. "We don't want to give the public the idea that we're tampering with anything sacred."

"Where's David Pringle?" Agnew inquired. "Couldn't he put his mind to it and enlist the academic community?"

"We've got him working on the Good News Hour expansion on the networks," Shakespeare reported.

"Get him."

Pringle was summoned to the presence of the communications *apparat*.

"How you doing, boy?" Agnew said, good-naturedly.

"Fine, Mr. President," Pringle said.

"You look a little tired—these characters working you too hard? I hear you've been doing a bang-up job on the script of the Spiro T. Agnew Physical Fitness segment."

"We think it's achieving results," Pringle said. "The American Medical Association people are surveying their doctors now and we hope to be able to have you report some good things."

"That's what we need—facts," Agnew said. "Now I've got a new little assignment for you. I want you to draft a speech for me on the Bill of Rights Revision Commission. The boys here will explain the details. Take a few days away from the office. And after that, you and I will have to start drafting my inaugural address. I know what I want to say but it may need polishing, Professor."

"I'll do my best, sir," Pringle said. And he added, "I hope you'll be able to block out some time to discuss your ideas with me alone. I'm a little better functioning that way instead of in a group."

The communicators detected nothing unusual in Pringle's request.

Pringle had decided to wait till the last possible moment before executing the K. Plan. Like many stunned people in the country, he could not believe that Spiro T. Agnew would actually be sworn in as President. He had felt the same way during the years of Nixon's active Presidency; but somehow Nixon was too obvious to be real, too much a national fixture as a candidate, too blatant in his stiff speeches and acts to be believable. Nixon was only a visitor in the White House, the Rotarian who came to dinner. He kept describing himself as "your President," as if saying it would make him so. Only his inadequacy and dysfunction gave him, finally, an unmasked human touch.

With Agnew the threat was real. He believed in his own sense of the rightness of everything he did. At the core was pride in personal appearance, brutishness, stamina, and discipline. He (Pringle observed) wanted to elevate his floorwalker life style to the cadences of a national religion. Till at least 1981, he would be a drill sergeant shaping up the government and people ruthlessly. He could turn out to be a Nixon with his fists punching. Seeing Agnew close up, Pringle's resolve became still stronger.

The escalation in Burma continued along the familiar lines of the Vietnam scenario. Pringle tried to learn more about it but he was not privy to the deliberations of the National Security Council. Even the White House staff was carefully checked. Nobody was permitted to remove documents from offices; the Secret Service guard had doubled to protect Agnew and the security of his decisions. Yet enough comings and goings were visible and enough hints dropped by Henry Kissinger's White

House warriors to indicate that real counterinsurgency and deeper involvement were in prospect after January 20, 1977.

The press blackout on Burma did not extend, however, to Joseph Alsop of the *Washington Post* syndicate who served as a conduit for whatever information the Pentagon and Kissinger's commandos planted. "The respect for the United States has soared from the Gulf of Siam to the Dardanelles as a result of certain diplomatic and military assurances," Alsop wrote on Christmas Day, 1976, in his finest geopolitical style from his command post in Georgetown. "I can report on the highest authority that the peasantry in the SEATO and CENTO states is delighted with the leadership now being displayed here in the nation's capital. In the final analysis, it is the show of iron will backed up by the flag and resources of a Great Power willing to assume the burden and the glory of Great Powerdom that will turn the tide against a philosophy rooted in worldwide terror and domination. From the Mekong Delta to the banks of the Ganges and Euphrates, the forces of freedom are locked in mortal combat for the minds and wills of hill and valley peoples. For two thousands years they have recognized that the Star of Bethlehem shines as a symbol of strength and moral fervor for men and nations in a symbiotic relationship to the indigenous religions of the fabled Far and Middle

East. I cite as but one example the support we are giving to General Ne Win and his Kaba Makyes, which readers of this pillar know means Our Free Homeland. The last time General Ne Win entertained your reporter in his beautiful villa that combines the best of the Oriental and Occidental worlds architecturally not to mention culinarily, he informed me that the IBM print-outs showed an ever-increasing number of areas safe from hostile interference. This was later confirmed to me by the Rand Corporation's study of rice harvests employing the latest agricultural advances introduced by American fertilizer technology. If we can win the rice baskets of the globe, we can attain a posture of respect among the peasantry that, in the long run, can form an invincible alliance against the forces of darkness."

Now President-elect Agnew could come out even more boldly in favor of the Greek colonels as the fulcrum of United States policy in the Mediterranean. "Enemies within and without this country attack the restoration of order in Greece," Agnew declared to the Association of Greek Shipowners in Boston. "It is time to recognize that there is an underlying mutuality of economic and political interests between the Old Republic of my ancestors and the New Republic that is America. We have much to give each other, much to learn from each other. I have in mind the press law approved by the Greek parliament recently. In spite of criticism by cer-

189

tain elements in the Council of Europe, that law guarantees freedom of expression there, except of course when deemed against the progress and programs of the State. At least in the Athens press we do not read diatribes against the American Seventh Fleet, against the Hilton Hotels in the islands and on the mainland, against the oil bottoms flying the American flag. Our Bill of Rights Revision Commission is now studying the Greek press law just as our Founding Fathers borrowed from the republican ideas of ancient Greece."

The linking of Greek and United States interests enabled several commentators in the press to interpret the historical significance of Agnew's remarks. In his *Foreign Affairs* editor's column, the ex-CIA operative, William Bundy, noted: "Looking over my diary notes for a certain day toward the end of December, 1949, I can now reveal that I was playing a round of golf with the King of all Greece, including of course the Peloponnesus, when he turned to me and suddenly said that Epicurus the Samian opposed the doctrine of Stoicism. I took this to mean that individual man is essentially selfish. Although Epicureanism has now become synonymous with a love of eating and drinking, with gluttony and the coarsest pleasures, when applied to nations there is a coda here for NATO and the future intercourse between Aristotle's Greece and Agnew's America. It is vital for nations to deal with each other in their own best interests; moral postures and lectures serve no purpose. Events since that by-now-historic round of golf have proved the King prescient."

The most unexpected of Agnew's actions in the foreign field was his proclamation permitting, for the first time in more than a decade, the importation of Havana cigars from Castro's Cuba. Some people said it was a way to retaliate at Canada—the main source of smuggled Havanas—for taking in American draft-age students by the tens of thousands and for allowing an anti-Agnew underground press to flourish there. Others thought it was purely a political move to put some one million fussy cigar smokers, fed up with the machine-made leaf from Tampa, in his debt. The negotiation was smoothed and sealed by Bebe Rebozo, Nixon's business associate, who had joined the Agnew camp following the indisposition of the President. In London, the *Observer* described the cigar proclamation as "Agnew's Bay of Pigs," seeing it as an effort to undermine the Castro regime that was doomed to failure. Nevertheless, the proclamation turned out to be the President-elect's first popular action.

His Cabinet was far more controversial. He presented the members personally—"Stand up and take a bow when I mention your name"—on the Good News Hour. "It is a great honor to introduce these members of the leadership community from all walks of life," Agnew said proudly. "McGeorge Bundy, who has vast experience safeguarding the security of these United States and making friends for us all over Southeast Asia, has consented to leave the Ford Foundation and join us as Secretary of State. Joseph Alsop, the internationally known columnist and expert on guerrilla counterinsurgency, has agreed to bring his great knowledge of military tactics to the government as our Secretary of Defense. I am creating a new Cabinet-level position for William F. Buckley, Jr., one of your favorite TV stars, as head of the USID—the United States Information Department—to tell it like it is to the American people just as the USIA, under Frank Shakespeare, tells it like it is to the foreigners overseas. On the distaff side, just to show you we're for the ladies, too, I am naming Ayn Rand, the brilliant economist of our way of life, to be Secretary of the Treasury. She believes in a day's pay for a day's work. I know everybody will be happy to hear that Robert Moses, who did such a swell job building the new beautiful bridge over Long Island Sound, will come out of retirement to help us build more new superhighways for the great American motorists and truckers as a can-do Secretary of Transportation. I am also pleased to announce that General William Westmoreland, a superb patriot who understands the needs of large bodies of men, will crown his career by becoming my Secretary of Labor. Harold E. Stassen, whose face may be familiar to you, declined to enter the primaries to run against yours truly, and I am glad he will be back in harness as head of Housing and Urban Development. Pat Moynihan, a man who knows his politics as well as what should and should not be allowed in the mailboxes of our land, is going to be my right-hand man as Postmaster General, where he will enforce the revised press-control laws. I know the police, the sheriffs, and the prosecutors will be happy to hear that Mayor Sam Yorty of Los Angeles, who believes in protecting the sanctity of our homes, will be the new Attorney General. We have the very distinguished John Connally of Texas in a key post—Secretary of the Interior—where he can keep an eye on the oil, natural gas, timber, and mining industries, and do what's right for their growth and development. And also from deep in the heart of Texas, Walt W. Rostow, who has a great deal of experience helping the farmers and peasants throughout Vietnam, Cambodia, and Laos and who knows his chemical herbicides, is going to be our Secretary of Agriculture. We have a most distinguished doctor with us who is leaving his very lucrative Park Avenue practice to join the team as head of the Health, Education and Welfare Department. Everybody knows his fourth cousin, Henry, my adviser on international security affairs who has done such a bang-up job preserving the peace, so now it's my pleasure to introduce the next

Secretary of HEW, Dr. Wolfgang Kissinger. Last but not least, you all remember Judge G. Harrold Carswell who was denied a seat on the Supreme Court despite his fine record as an independent thinker? Well, we're bringing the Judge aboard with the Agnew crew to help steer the ship of state as your new Secretary of Commerce. He and the other good folks here are pledged to do their best and give their all for a better break for the businessman and the workingman, for a better economy, for making haste slowly in safeguarding private and property rights, and for an end to the squishy-soft thinking of the past so that the nations of the world will really know that the U.S.A. deserves and demands new respect. Thank you and good night, neighbors."

After watching the presentation of the Agnew Cabinet on the Good News Hour, David Pringle took out the old-fashioned Waterman pen, inserted the powder-filled cartridge, and placed it inside his coat jacket carefully.

CHAPTER 9

January 20, 1977

ON THE evening before the day that Spiro T. Agnew would be sworn in as President of the United States, the man who planned to stop him reread the paragraphs he had contributed to the inaugural address and at the same time watched a television program on all three networks called, "A Tour of the White House with Judy Agnew."

The commentator with her on the preempted two hours was none other than the new Secretary of the USID, William F. Buckley, Jr., now the most powerful journalist in the country.

"Here we are in the very room where Dolley Madison once swayed the course of empire, so to speak," Buckley emoted, "and on this very gold service she dined with her husband and the leaders of the new nation. I wonder what your feelings of apotheosis are the day before moving in?"

"Oh," said the pleasant First Lady, looking confused.

"I'm scared to break anything so we're bringing in our own dishes."

"And now we move to the East Room where you and your husband, the President, will preside over affairs of state. History will look down upon you, and you are dichotomously reminded of—"

"It reminds me of when I went to work in the Maryland Casualty Company as a file clerk and Ted says he tripped over me there. He worked in the adjustments department and when he asked to see the claims on file he always asked for me and that's how I first met him and after we were married we spent our honeymoon at the Hotel Emerson, in downtown Baltimore."

"It certainly sounds romantic," Buckley said, rolling his tongue and his eyes. "Allow me to interrupt this fascinating narrative for a brief word from our sponsor, Dr Pepper, and we'll continue in a moment."

After four more commercials, Buckley and the First Lady arrived in the President's Oval Office to sum up the program for the captive audience of seventy-five million Americans.

"For the next four years the lives and destinies of the people will be determined from here," Buckley said. "What do you envision for the plethora of events writ large in annum 1977?"

"I don't take stands on anything—I stay out of the political end of it," Mrs. Agnew said. "Whenever I'm

asked what subject I've majored in, I say that I've
majored in marriage. I think we'll enjoy living here once
we get used to all the rooms and I sincerely hope everybody enjoys having my husband as their President."

"Graciously put," said the grinning Secretary of the
USID, licking his teeth. "Thank you for letting us into
your new home for this 'Tour of the White House with
Judy Agnew' and, penultimately, for permitting the
American public to share your most refreshing ideas,
thanks to Dr Pepper."

The Secret Service men appeared nervous and cau-
tious when David Pringle arrived at the White House
early the next morning. They stopped him at the entrance instead of waving him on as they had done for
months. Pringle felt his stomach churning; he wondered
if they would detect anything different about his face
and manner.

"We have you down on the list for the White House
staff on the Capitol steps," a Secret Service man said.
"You'll have to wear this blue button around here today
and at the inauguration. It's a precaution."

"Anything up?" Pringle said, casually.

"The usual rumors and nut calls," the Secret Service
man said. "The President-elect is in his office. He left
orders to send you right in, professor."

"Thanks," Pringle said. "See you later."

It's going to happen now, he thought; I'm really going to do it; I must keep my hand steady.

When he entered the President-elect's office, Agnew appeared ready to depart even though the inauguration was two hours away. The future President was dressed in a cutaway and Pringle suddenly remembered a bloated penguin in a Marx Brothers movie. Agnew was working over his inaugural address with his top hat on.

"I want you to listen to the delivery of your paragraphs and see if I come across with the right resonance in my voice," Agnew said. "If there is anything that bugs me, it's being ridiculed by your friends in the colleges and universities, the snobs who think they have a first mortgage on the English language."

Pringle nodded and moved closer. Nobody else was in the Oval office.

Agnew stood up and started to read aloud:

"The greatest enemies of effective, intelligent government are opportunists who have learned that a measure of popularity can be cheaply purchased by assuming oversimplified positions on complex issues. Many people turn to the half-truths of the lunatic fringe who proudly identify themselves as so-called liberals. Unreasonable ultimatums of power-crazed integrationist leaders are accepted as dogma—but let me make my position absolutely clear now for the next four years.

"Open-occupancy legislation, the attempted crashing

of private membership clubs, unlawful trespassing and unlawful demonstrating, violate the civil rights of the Negro himself. For social acceptance can never be legislated because it is the voluntary acceptance of one man by another as a companion, not the acceptance by one race of another in theory, that counts. The great freedoms we enjoy in this country must be newly delineated for a new era or we shall perish. I believe in freedom of selection, freedom of association, freedom in the marketplace, and freedom for the government. I pledge here and now to work for these as the new four freedoms."

Agnew looked up for approval.

"It's got moxie when you read it yourself," Pringle said, hearing the incredible phrases he had been assigned to write.

"Now let me skip along here to the foreign stuff," Agnew said. He leafed through the pages and continued aloud again:

"My Administration will not draw a blueprint for the first defeat and denigration of the United States in our history. While I do not question the patriotism of those who would have us abandon our commitments to friends and allies in Asia, I do deeply question their judgment and their right to hold office.

"If we slink home, defeated and ridiculed, from the battlefield, from the seas and skies we now dominate, what will be the reaction of true Americans when they wake up to learn that thousands of lives and billions in taxes were spent only to find national humiliation and disaster at the end of the road? One wonders if those who would allow this to happen really give a damn.

"Well, my fellow Americans and fellow veterans, your President, like his illustrious predecessor, Richard M. Nixon, really does give a damn about the prestige and honor of the United States and we will expose and up-root those elements resisting this new administration."

Pringle felt his heart pounding.

Agnew started to walk back to his desk, proud of himself and his language. Halfway there, he stopped to adjust his ascot and stretch the thick skin in his neck in front of a closet mirror. He stepped back a few feet to admire himself full-length in his inaugural costume.

"You think it'll go over all right, then?" Agnew asked.

Not in the back, Pringle said to himself. When he turns. I want him to see me plain. As myself, David Pringle, who once had the courage in another country in another time.

"There's a small change I'd like to offer," Pringle said, softly, as he had planned to say it. "It's necessary to get my point over to you."

He heard footsteps outside and a voice calling to Agnew, "Mr. *President*." A proud secretary's voice.

Pringle unscrewed the pen's cap. It didn't matter any

more. As Agnew turned to face him, he pointed the innocent-looking weapon at the President-elect. For an instant the ignited powder popped like a firecracker and flashed a yellow-orange flame. It grazed and discolored Agnew's spotless stiff shirtfront; but he was unharmed.

The secretary screamed. Two Secret Service men rushed in and, seeing the smoking pen in Pringle's hand, had a choice of disarming him or killing him. Durham and Licata had tried, but these men justified their most terrible expectations. They did not play games. They pumped bullets into Pringle's chest. Without a word he slumped and fell, the first and last critic of the new Administration.

CHAPTER 10

An Old Republic

FOLLY AND ignorance are a sort of emptiness of the soul. There is the dissembler, who harangues a multitude in public. Is he the statesman or the demagogue? The demagogue.

—Plato's *Republic* and *Sophist*

O kind missionary, O compassionate missionary, leave China! Come home and convert these Christians!

—Mark Twain's *On the United States*

The funny thing is, Richard Nixon and Spiro Agnew really thought they were the President and Vice President of the United States.

—Mitgang's *Presumptuous Pensées*